A MESSAGE FROM CHICKEN HOUSE

Kiran is a master storyteller and every one of her novels is beautiful in its own way. For me, *A Secret of Birds & Bone* is her most colourful and unusual story yet. Here she weaves a mystery of bones, belief and plague; a mystery which feels like it really *matters* – for beneath it is a truth of love, family, friendship and magic. Like everything Kiran writes, this story is full of layers – and what you think you know, or guess, turns out to be so much more than you could ever have imagined! Can you *unlock* the truth? (That's a clue!) Brilliant.

BARRY CUNNINGHAM
Publisher
Chicken House

A
SECRET
OF
BIRDS
& BONE

Kiran Millwood Hargrave

Chicken House

2 Palmer Street, Frome, Somerset BA11 1DS
www.chickenhousebooks.com

Text © Kiran Millwood Hargrave 2020

First published in Great Britain in 2020
This edition published 2021
Chicken House
2 Palmer Street
Frome, Somerset BA11 1DS
United Kingdom
www.chickenhousebooks.com

Chicken House/Scholastic Ireland, 89E Lagan Road, Dublin Industrial Estate,
Glasnevin, Dublin D11 HP5F, Republic of Ireland

Kiran Millwood Hargrave has asserted her right under the Copyright, Designs
and Patents Act 1988 to be identified as the author of this work.

Cover and interior design by Helen Crawford-White
Typeset by Dorchester Typesetting Group Ltd
Printed and bound in Great Britain by CPI Group (UK) Ltd, Croydon CR0 4YY

FSC
www.fsc.org
MIX
Paper from
responsible sources
FSC® C020471

3 5 7 9 10 8 6 4

British Library Cataloguing in Publication data available.

PB ISBN 978-1-913322-96-0
eISBN 978-1-913322-63-2

For my editor, Rachel Leyshon,
for the glittering lessons & shining structures,
& all the other treasures you have taught me

Other children's books by
Kiran Millwood Hargrave:

The Girl of Ink & Stars
The Island at the End of Everything
The Way Past Winter
The Deathless Girls

And for adults:

The Mercies

1

In the grounds of a ruined monastery, on the outskirts of Siena, a girl awoke in a charnel house.

All about her were skeletons: by the thin shafts of light flitting in from the slits in the ribcage shutters she could see the bed about her, built from tibias and fibulas. A moon-white skull still warm from last night's fire was cupped over her feet, for here the nights were clear and cool. Over her head draped a canopy of gold-dipped toe bones in great, gilded wreaths, and teeth were set like stars in the chinks in the walls.

But the girl was not afraid. This house, built of old and golden bone, was her home – and today was her twelfth birthday.

No one else was awake: her mother's and

brother's beds along the other walls were still, and the house was silent as a tomb. Sofia lay calm in her bone bed, and smiled. Soon Corvith, their crow, would squawk for breakfast, and her brother Ermin, always tired and sleeping long into mornings, would grumble at the noise, and Mamma would rise and stoke the fire for lavender honey and milk. There would be presents, and perhaps Mamma would change her mind about letting them go to the Palio—

Thump.

Sofia stopped smiling. She sat up, and immediately bumped her head on the headboard. She had lately grown too tall for her bed, and Mamma hadn't yet made it bigger.

Thump.

She got up more slowly, rubbing the sore spot on her crown, and turned towards the closed door that led to their mother's workshop.

Thump.

The sound came again, followed by small clinks, light as raindrops stumbling against the tiles of the patella roof. Now that her eyes were adjusted to the gloom, Sofia could see the door was slightly ajar and that her mother's bed was empty.

Heaviness flooded her body, like she hadn't slept at all. She'd hoped these days were over. The days where Mamma seemed to float through her waking hours as though under a storm cloud, or crushed beneath an invisible sack of weighty worry. Mamma had promised they would be done, only yesterday.

I'm finished, she said last night, pressing a kiss to Sofia's forehead, *no more late nights. No more days away. It ends tomorrow, and we will celebrate your birthday like a saint's day.*

Sofia clenched her teeth together until her jaw clicked. Mamma had lied to her, and on her birthday of all days. She pushed back her blanket and padded on bare, quiet feet past Ermin's bed and Mamma's empty sheets to the gap in the door.

Corvith stirred as she passed, snug in his skull nest.

'So?' he squawked, but a quick rub of his feathered head sent his beady black eye closed again, and Sofia was able to peer unnoticed through the door that connected the bedroom and Mamma's workroom. This was as far as she was allowed to go, now.

The shutters here were closed too, and a lavender wax candle burnt in its knucklebone holder, wafting the purple scent towards Sofia. Mamma was hunched at her broad worktable, surrounded by creamy white bone shavings. Her dark skin was streaked pale with the powdery dust that settled finely in the air about her, her black curls caught up away from her face with a finger-bone hairpin.

This was the first thing Sofia had ever made, a simple design where she'd hinged the joint with bronze so it could manage Mamma's unruly tangles. Ermin could have made better, and it was a trinket compared to Mamma's artistry, but still Mamma treasured it like the finest relic.

Sofia knew not to be jealous of the hours Mamma spent in this room, the door pushed to or closed entirely, because Mamma had a calling, a skill, a *gift*, and such things were valuable and must not be ignored.

Mamma was an ossuarist, a bone builder. She was the greatest in all of Italy, perhaps in all the world, though there were rumours from Central Asia of a man who crafted carts and boats.

But the delicacy of Mamma's creations was unparalleled. Ermin and Sofia watched as she wove thigh bone with clavicle as though they were lace, frosted knuckles with diamonds to make hinges that would never break, made gold-dipped locks from vertebrae that could be opened only by a finger bone from the same skeleton.

She specialized in reliquaries – ornate bone boxes to hold the famous relics of the cathedral. These remains of saints were believed to have the power of healing. Santa Maria's toe bone, said to cure dancing manias, was encased in a lattice of ankle bones. Santa Peter's jawbone, healer of toothache, was tiled in molars. Her greatest work was for Santa Catherine's finger bone, said to heal the sicknesses of whoever held it in their bare palm. This received a particularly fine gold-filigree box, with an especially complex lock of knuckles.

Mamma also made simpler boxes for poorer customers, as well as earrings, door handles and sometimes, like their bone house, whole rooms.

Mamma's skills were celebrated, but very few knew her truest gift. Only Sofia, Ermin and Corvith knew – and not even they were allowed to watch the process. Only they knew that their mamma was not solely a bone builder: she was a bone binder. When she made something, it was not merely beautiful. It was blessed. Blessed by the spirit of the person whose bones had been used to make it. Some might call it magic but Mamma thought that made it sound like superstition, in the realms of fairies and witches. And this particular magic was bone-bound, earth-made, rule-tangled.

So when a widow brought her husband's rib to become a brooch worn over her heart, she would be comforted in her weeping by the double beat of a ghostly pulse worn against her chest. When a bootmaker brought her the skeleton of a beloved assistant to make into a coat rack, it was the manservant's spirit that reached out to take their master's worries even as his finger bones held the cloak.

Even before the smallpox, Mamma took great care over the cleaning of the bones in the well before binding, and Sofia helped. Always it took place at dawn, in the orange tinge of the world coming awake, washing her mother and the bones in golden light.

Then the smallpox came. Ermin fell sick with it, and for a while Sofia was worried because Mamma seemed so desperate. A doctor came, and left looking helpless. But Ermin was well again within a week, thanks to Mamma. They took him to the well one morning to make him better, and he recovered. But after that, Mamma refused to work for anyone but herself, and Sofia and Ermin were forbidden from touching the bones.

If only Mamma let her help with the work again, Sofia would be content to live just the four of them on the monastery hill – Mamma, Ermin, Corvith and she – for the rest of her days.

That was until a year ago.

A year ago, a stranger visited their house and Sofia finally came to understand that light must be followed by dark.

That good is sometimes chased, hard and merciless as hunting dogs, by bad.

2

S ofia had been spying that day.

She and Ermin were playing on the hillside beside their house, late into the evening. Since Mamma had stopped taking commissions, their days stretched into long, unformed expanses of time, wide as the views from the top of the hill. The ruins of the monastery crouched at the base, and the olive grove grew right to the crown where their well was.

The grove was planted when the monks still lived there and made olive oil, and olive bread, and olive soap, and so many things from olives Mamma called them the Order of the Olive.

Beneath the hill was a river: one of the under-ground rivers that criss-crossed Siena like hidden seams, none reaching the surface. They were buried so deep Sofia would not have believed they existed if the water didn't come up from the well, cool and clear, in their bucket each day.

Fed by sunlight and this hidden river, the olive trees were overgrown and knotting into each other, so close and inscrutable it made Sofia wonder if all wild things would reach for each other if only they were allowed to.

Their world had shrunk to this grove. Mamma was sure that the smallpox still lingered on the streets of Siena and she had forbidden them going further than the monastery boundary, marked by an ancient, twisted tree. Sofia's memories of the city had the quality of dreams — faded as old cloth but soft and comforting to the touch.

Still, Sofia and Ermin didn't much mind that Siena was off limits. It was magical when the silvery leaves were at their thickest, the olives hanging black and salty-sweet, and you could easily get lost in the warren of curving branches, especially in the dark. But Ermin and Sofia had grown up here, knew the routes like their own hands and could always find their way to the top, to the small well sunk into the crest.

They rarely came home until long after dusk, allowing their mamma to work in peace. That evening, Sofia's mouth was smarting from the salt of the olives, and she had a sudden hankering for the strawberries that grew small and sweet in the bonemeal-fed soil outside their home. She left Ermin throwing olives in the air for Corvith and wove her way down to the charnel house.

She emerged from the shadowy grove into the bruised navy of night, but something caught light and tossed it into her eyes. Before her, in a silver harness and with a high plume, was a white horse. It was tied to the post in front of their house, bright as the moon.

Could it be possible Mamma was with a customer, at last?

The horse lifted its head from the strawberry bushes and, though Sofia knew it was not possible, seemed to glare at her. She decided to let the horse have the strawberries from the bush, and instead eat the slightly soft ones they'd collected to make jam. She edged carefully around the horse, steering well clear of its powerful hind legs, and slipped quietly inside the house so as not to disturb

Mamma with the visitor.

The house was as cool as the grove, its moonish glow impervious to the temperature outside, be it too hot or too cold. The door of Mamma's workshop was ajar, leaking candlelight, and Sofia kept to the wall, skirting towards the bowl of red fruit on the table.

A squawk brought her up short. She froze, wondering if Corvith had followed and was about to give her away, but then the sound came again and she could place it as coming from inside Mamma's workshop.

It was harsher than Corvith's caw, with the edge of metal set beneath. A magpie's caw. Her mamma's guest must be one of the duchessa's guards, for they alone had command of the birds that circled the city day and night.

Her teeth set on edge. The magpies never seemed right to her. There was something in their eyes that was a little too sharp, a little too calculating. Almost human. They seemed to see everything, know everything.

Sofia edged closer to the door, curious to see a guard up close. Perhaps he had brought a clavicle from his dead lover to be made into a scabbard, or a finger for a key. Perhaps Mamma would at last start accepting work from the city again.

Keeping her body pressed to the wall, Sofia peered inside. The first thing she saw was the magpie. It was huge and hooded in silver mesh, like a hawk, which was why it didn't see her. Its talons were filigreed in precious metal and it perched not on the shoulder of a guard, but a woman.

She was tall and turned towards Mamma, so Sofia could not see her face. She was clad in a beautiful silver cloak that shimmered like water. The stranger reached up to soothe her magpie, who obviously sensed Sofia's presence.

'Hush, Orsa.' Elegant wrists showed slim against the lace of her cuffs. Her hair was hidden beneath the net of a silver veil. The magpie settled, snapping its beak.

'As I was saying,' said the woman, in a low voice. 'This is less an offer, and more an order.'

'And if I refuse?' Mamma's voice was taut with something Sofia had never heard in it before. Fear.

'Do you forget who you are talking to?'

Mamma fell silent.

'I only mean to remind you of certain facts,' continued the woman. 'Perhaps your children would like to know what their mother has done – or the people of Siena . . .'

'Please.' Mamma swallowed. 'I can't.'

'You're the only one who can. You will not go unrewarded.' There was a clink, and Sofia saw a silver pouch drop on to Mamma's worktable. 'Tomorrow, you start.'

Deaf to Mamma's pleas, the woman hoisted the magpie higher on her slender shoulder and turned for the door.

Sofia stumbled backwards, crouching beneath the table with its coarse woven cloth. The bone floor hard beneath her knees, she shrank down until she saw the stranger's shoes. Peeking out from her glistening dress, they were embroidered so intricately they looked like lace on her feet. A smell, herbal and clean, like the peppermint poultices Mamma used to soothe insect bites, followed her.

Sofia stayed crouched under the table until she heard Mamma fling her workshop door closed, sending bone dust drifting from the ribcage rafters. Crawling out, she regarded the door with its familiar bone hinges and handle, and wondered if she could go inside and ask Mamma outright about the visitor. But then the moment passed.

Sofia went back outside, strawberries forgotten. The light was low, but still she was just in time to see moonlight dance across the silver-clad figure on a white horse, a magpie swooping overhead.

3

In the days and months following the stranger's visit, their little life changed. Or rather, Mamma did. They were still forbidden to go to the city, but now the workroom was off limits too. Sofia would have minded less had Mamma been happy, but her moods descended thick and cold as winter fog.

Sofia sometimes thought it was her fault, that she should have opened Mamma's workroom door that day, thrown her arms around Mamma and told her that whatever the stranger wanted from her, she didn't have to bear it alone. But she hadn't, and so Mamma moved as though under a storm cloud, constantly in fear of silver lightning striking.

Until today, thought Sofia, watching the top of Mamma's head through the gap. *Mamma promised it would end today.* From today, there would be no more secrecy, no more storm clouds. Mamma would start singing while she worked again. *Today was meant to be the end*.

Sofia's frustration made her bold. It was her birthday. She was twelve now, and Mamma should not treat her like a child. She was going to make Mamma tell her what she had been working on all this time.

Sofia took a deep breath and pushed open the door. The workroom's well-oiled toe-bone hinges never squeaked but still Mamma wheeled around the moment Sofia crossed the threshold, so accustomed to the space she could sense the slightest change in the air.

It had been months since Sofia had entered, but it was the same as she remembered. It was the largest room of the two that comprised their home. The walls were lined with shelves that held bones in the way rich people might have books – a library of mandibles, tarsals, fibias and patellas, arranged by size.

The room curved slightly, mimicking the natural cadence of its building parts – as Mamma always said, *There are no straight lines in the body*, and so, aside from doors, there were no straight lines in their home. The furnace radiated heat in one corner and her tools were kept in the cooling bucket beside it, full of fresh well water. It used to be Sofia's job to draw the water and to scatter it on the bones once Mamma had finished working, but no longer. Seeing it now, she felt again how fiercely she missed working with Mamma.

'Invited yourself in, have you?' Mamma's voice was unreadable, flat as a puddle.

Sofia stepped towards the worktable, jaw set, and was just about to begin her interrogation when she saw Mamma's face was not wan and strained as was usual these days, but lit by a huge smile.

'Good morning, *piccolina*.' She shifted so Sofia could not see what was on the table.

'I'm not a little one,' said Sofia, crossing her arms and trying to peer around her mother's body. 'I'm twelve.'

'Ah, but you've caught me finishing a present I made for my little one,' said Mamma smilingly, brown eyes twinkling as she nonchalantly adjusted her hairpin. 'If you are too grown up for it—'

'No,' said Sofia, failing to hide her excitement. 'You can give it to me.'

Mamma laughed, and it was her old laugh.

She made such beautiful things. For Sofia's tenth birthday, a calendar candle that burnt down into a miniature bone box in which Sofia kept small treasures like shells. For Ermin's eighth, a clock-work squirrel skeleton that chattered and peeled shavings of candied fruit with its teeth.

Last year, on her eleventh birthday, Sofia had received her greatest treasure: the canopy of gilded toe bones that hung like a glittering chain over her bed. She did not see how Mamma could outdo herself this year.

Sofia held out her hands, eyes squeezed tightly shut. Into them Mamma placed something so light, it felt like a feather.

'Happy birthday, *piccolina*.'

Sofia looked down at a chain of interlinked coils of bone, finely wrought to the point Sofia barely felt it, though she could see it rested in her hands. On the end was a bone locket, fashioned into the shape of the cathedral tower. Though Sofia had not been to the cathedral for years, she saw this tower every day from the hill. It was so high it seemed to stand almost level with their hilltop, even at a distance. She recognized it instantly, with its stripes and crenellated edges. This version was half the size of her palm and looked delicate as a wafer.

When Sofia took it, she felt something wash through her – a calm like when she stroked Corvith, or hugged Mamma, or sat on their well watching over the world. A feeling like coming home.

'It's beautiful.'

Mamma closed Sofia's hand about it. 'And it matters, Sofia. Keep it safe, always.'

'I promise.' She hugged Mamma, breathing her in. Mamma made her own lavender oil from the purple bushes that grew large and fragrant outside their house, and would rub it into her dark skin until it shone. She also washed her thick black curls with lavender water, so she always smelt beautiful. In summer, the bone walls of their house hummed with bees, as though their ribcage struts still held breath. 'Thank you.'

To think of her mother, so sad and sunk inside herself lately, still finding time to make something so lovely – it made her chest hurt.

Mamma caught the tears in her voice and held

Sofia more tightly to her. 'I'm sorry,' she mumbled into the top of her head. 'I've not been myself. I've had to . . . But that's over now. Today, it ends.'

There was an enquiring chitter and a moment later Corvith wiggled his way into the middle of the hug, burrowing into Sofia's hair and then Mamma's.

'So-so!' he said, in his croaky crow voice. Mamma drew back and smiled down at them.

'Morning, Corvith. Come, *piccolina*. We'll wake your brother and then we can have milk and honey for breakfast. Then,' a shadow crossed her face, 'I'll go to Siena. And *then* your birthday can begin. I'll have another gift for you when I return. A more precious gift.'

'But this is enough,' protested Sofia, unable to think of what could be better than the locket. 'What is it?'

'The truth,' said Mamma in a soft voice.

Sofia felt a fizz of excitement. 'What truth?'

'Later,' said Mamma. 'First, I must go to the city.'

'Can I come?' said Sofia, hoping against hope that today was the day Mamma's ban would lift. 'It's the Palio, for the first time in years, and I've never seen it—'

'No.' Mamma was already distracted, moving past her to the sleeping shape of Ermin. She rested a hand to his forehead, as she did each morning, as though some sickness might still linger in his blood. 'It's best to stay here.'

They woke a grumbling Ermin and had a breakfast of lavender honey in milk, and black bread with more honey. Ermin gave her his usual gift, a small square of stitched cloth embroidered with something that made him think of her. It was a strawberry this time.

'Because you ate them all this year,' he said accusingly. He'd been making these patchwork squares since he could hold a needle and thread, and one day Sofia would have enough to make a quilt. 'Just like the year before, and the one before that.'

Sofia stuck out her tongue to mask her discomfort at the memory of the white horse standing before their house, stripping the fruit from the bushes.

'It's lovely, Ermin,' said Mamma, gesturing for Sofia to thank him. She did so, and hugged him briefly. His body was thin beneath his clothes. Since the smallpox, he had never recovered his plump glow.

'Thanks, Ermin,' she said, meaning it a lot more than she seemed to. It didn't do to show little brothers how much their gifts meant.

Mamma sighed and hauled herself to her feet, as though she were a hundred years old and ached all over. She went into her workshop and emerged with a bundle small enough to slip into a pocket. But she held it instead, carefully, as though what was inside was either very delicate or very dangerous.

'What's that, Mamma?' asked Ermin and, to Sofia's surprise, she answered.

'A reliquary,' she said, flipping back the cloth to show them. It was beautiful; a tiny box built of toe and finger bones cross-hatched and shot through with silver. 'The last one.'

'Really?' asked Sofia. Many years ago, Mamma had told her one of her life's ambitions was to create such a box for each of the eighty-seven saint's relics in the cathedral. Was this what she had been working on? But Mamma didn't explain, only sighed and rewrapped the box.

'I'll only be a couple of hours,' she said. 'As quick

as I can. Send Corvith to check outside if anyone knocks.'

Ermin went to lock the door when Mamma left, but Sofia put her hand on his. 'Leave it.'

'But Mamma said—'

'That she'll be a couple of hours. And it's nearly eight o'clock.'

'So?'

'The Palio starts at nine.'

Ermin bit his lip worriedly. 'But—'

'But nothing,' said Sofia, throwing on her cape – the one with a hood, so she could hide her face if necessary. 'You coming, or not?'

4

The Palio was the most ancient and challenging horse race in all of Italy, and maybe in all the world.

There were ten horses with ten riders, all representing a different district. They would each begin at their own corner of the city and charge through the streets before convening in the main square, the Piazza del Campo. The first to complete three laps won.

Sofia could only imagine it, because she had never been allowed to attend.

'When you're old enough, you can go,' Mamma had said, but refused to tell her what age this might be. 'I'll know,' she said vaguely. And no matter how old and wise and tall Sofia tried to appear, so far, she had no luck.

All she'd ever seen of the Palio was the view from their hill. She remembered watching the *bandiere delle contrade* – the banners of each district – flying from the palazzo a week before: the blue and white of the *Onda*, the wave, representing the carpenters; the white circle and red stitches of the *Nicchio*, the seashell, that flew over the potters; the shoemakers chanting beneath the red-and-black *Civetta*, the owl. Even these she knew only as a distant memory, from before the pox. But last week they had appeared again, signalling the Duchessa of Siena was ready to let life return to normal. Sofia only wished Mamma agreed with their leader.

There was no sign of Mamma on the path to town, though they had not left so far behind her. Butterflies with steel wings flung themselves around Sofia's stomach, her heart pounding like horses' hooves with nerves and excitement at her own daring. Ermin was still protesting, his brown curls stuck to the side of his face where they had pressed against his pillow.

'We really shouldn't,' he muttered breathlessly, as Corvith circled lazily above them on hot air currents. 'We'll be in such trouble. What about the smallpox?'

'It was years ago,' said Sofia, wishing he'd stayed behind if all he was going to do was complain. When he'd been sick he hadn't spoken at all, his mouth so dry Sofia had to use a sponge to drip water between his lips. She shuddered, pushing away the memory and feeling her irritation return. He was so slow and, though she knew it was because his illness had weakened him, she couldn't help but feel annoyed.

'So why doesn't Mamma let us visit?'

Sofia, having no answer, snapped instead. 'Go back then.'

He settled into a sulk as they approached the boundary of the city. Unwilling to hesitate and give Ermin an opportunity to suggest going home, Sofia plunged blindly onwards, trusting that soon enough they would encounter the crowds flocking to the Palio.

Their route took them first through the narrow alleys of the shoemaker district, the smell of tanning leather coming bitter as old lemons on her tongue. The steaming pits where the leather was soaked were as full as ever though their usual attendants were absent, as they would have been during the time of smallpox.

Mamma, Sofia and Ermin had been mostly protected from the darkness of those days, their charnel house a refuge from the graveyard their city became. Ermin was sick for a few nights, but Sofia had never truly imagined he was in danger. Mamma had nursed him well, and he had no scars. Only the tiredness, and the thinness of his face and body.

Others were not so lucky. The Duke of Siena, Duc Machelli, had declared quarantine in the city before he himself died of the sickness, and his wife, Duchessa Serafina Machelli, a famous beauty, had carried on his good works by building a new convent to care for sick or orphaned children. She must have loved him very much, as she was still in mourning and no longer seen outside the palazzo. Since she still made ample provision for the hospital and orphanage, there was little fuss that their leader had turned invisible.

Sofia and Ermin broke out of the warren that edged the city and into the wider, cleaner streets of the dressmakers' district. Everything smelt of the rosemary and lavender the clothes were packed in to keep the moths at bay. Here the houses were wider and shorter and had real glass in the windows. Sofia glanced up at them as they passed; no one waved when she did. The faces in the windows were drawn and pale.

'Mamma didn't lie about no children allowed,' murmured Ermin, as they were squashed against a narrow alley wall by the crushing crowd. 'There aren't any.'

Sofia looked around. He was right – clearly the citizens of Siena agreed that only adults should attend the Palio. A few people stared openly at them and whispered to each other. Sofia pulled up her cloak's hood and drew Ermin into her side as they pushed further into Siena's heart, willing no one to send them away.

Wells were set in the middle of each square they passed, like beads on a necklace. At each one the crush deepened, with people standing in long lines around them.

'Is there no water?' whispered Ermin, as they watched a woman draw up her bucket only half full of murky liquid.

'Shhh,' said Sofia, like she always did when she just didn't know the answer to Ermin's questions. It certainly seemed like water was scarce here, though at their well at home it came up pure and sweet each morning.

By the time they wove their way into the city centre, dirt hardened beneath their feet, the sun was strong and the air still – full of the smells and shouts of people as they listened for the trumpet that signalled the start of the race. Sofia had heard it even from her hilltop in long-past years, and couldn't wait to be there in person to hear the sound.

Corvith settled in his skull sling as the crowds swelled, snapping his beak bad-temperedly if anyone brushed against him. As they squeezed down a final narrow and stepped alley, leading to the Piazza del Campo where the riders would converge for the final laps, Ermin was also not happy.

'We shouldn't be here,' he said for the tenth time, and Sofia rolled her eyes at her little brother. 'It's too hot.'

Sofia looked around, searching for somewhere to buy him something to drink. But all she could see were taverns – water seemed to be in very short supply. 'Not long now. We can have a lemon ice when we get home.'

'I feel funny.' He did look flushed. 'And people keep looking at us.'

Sofia could not disagree with him there. She'd been forced by the heat to take off her cloak, and the sun and stares were burning the back of her neck. Had her locket been made of metal it would have scalded her skin, and her sandals chafed from the walk into town. They were surrounded by jostling people who, despite the early hour, smelt of sharp wine. Sofia wondered if this was because of the queue for the wells, or because today was a celebration.

She wished Mamma were with them, and that she could ask her all these questions. Sofia stood on tiptoe. The black-and-white blocks of the cathedral loomed in the near distance, its spires the closest thing to heaven in the whole city. Magpies spiralled around its stone.

Sofia felt for her locket, an echo of the cathedral tower, and held it up before her. They were a perfect match, aside from a little notch in one side of the locket. Sofia had not noticed this detail before and she eyed it, frowning.

'What is it?' asked Ermin.

'Looks like a keyhole.' Sofia squinted in the bright sunlight and noticed the tiny seam where the locket could open. Mamma must have forgotten to give her the key. It was so perfect that, were she able to open it, she wouldn't be surprised if miniature magpies the size of mosquitoes flew out.

The second-highest tower in the city stood across from them. It was part of the palazzo, and comets of wheeling magpies spun around it. The many *contrade*, flags of the citizens, hung limp from its shining honey-gold stone. Atop the magpie tower was rumoured to be a prison cell where the worst criminals of the city were kept.

'Welcome, my dear citizens!' A voice, low and musical, seemed to boom out of the air itself. 'Soon the Palio shall begin!'

A mighty cheer flew up from the crowd like a flock of birds, and a woman beside them did a little jig in excitement. Sofia squinted, but couldn't see anyone on the palazzo steps.

'Was that the duchessa?' Ermin asked, craning his neck. 'Where is she?'

31

'I'd stay out of sight if I were you,' said the jigging woman. She had stopped dancing and was staring at Ermin and Sofia. 'Where's your mother?'

'There,' said Sofia, gesturing vaguely. 'But where's the duchessa?'

The woman was still peering at them closely. 'It's the pipes.'

'Pipes?' repeated Sofia.

'The pipes.' The woman pointed at the palazzo. Sofia followed her finger and saw an array of pale tubes running around the walls of the palace, like fine vines. 'Pipes from the palace. The latest style apparently. The King of Copenhagen has some for music, so he can hear it in rooms where he isn't. Our duchessa went one better. Got them so she can speak to us without breaking her mourning confinement by leaving the palace.'

'Pipes,' murmured Sofia, this time to herself. She had never heard of such a thing.

'Move up!'

Sofia felt a push, and they were shunted further towards the piazza. She tightened her grip on Ermin, and Corvith's sling, and hoped they'd picked a safe place to stand.

'There's no room!' came a returning cry from ahead, but the people behind, emptying out of a nearby tavern, were stronger. As she kept a firm hold of her brother's hand, slippery with sweat, they were forced out of the alley and into the piazza itself.

'Back!' shouted a guard, his magpie's beak glinting cruelly on his shoulder. 'The Palio is about to begin!'

But Sofia and Ermin were no match for the people trying to shove their way to the front. Ermin lost his footing, and spilt past the barrier and on to the racetrack.

5

'**B**ack I say!' The guard aimed a kick at the dirt beside Ermin's head.

'Ermin!' Sofia tried to yank him to safety but couldn't reach. She tried to slip under the barrier, but many hands held her still.

'You mustn't,' said the woman. 'If you're orphans, they'll take you away.'

'We're not! That's my brother,' she said, shrugging loose. Corvith took flight and swooped towards Ermin, trying to help. The guard's magpie snipped the air with its beak, chattering aggressively, but it was held in place by a silver lead about its ankle.

As the birds sniped at each other, Sofia was able to grasp hold of Ermin's arm and pull him roughly back to the relative safety of the crowd.

'You must be more careful,' she hissed, dusting her brother down and soothing Corvith who had returned to his skull nest. 'You could have been hurt.'

'It wasn't my fault,' Ermin whined, as the palazzo doors opened with a mighty *bang*.

Everyone turned towards the sound, cheering. Sofia imagined the duchessa might be about to arrive, to start the race, or perhaps a trumpeter in her stead. But from the mighty door came not the elusive duchessa, nor a trumpeter but . . .

'Mamma!'

Sofia's cry was lost to the stifling air. But it *was* their mother, unmistakable with her wild black hair and wilder eyes, running as fast as she could, sunlight glinting off her hairpin. The crowd jeered as she tripped down the steps. Two guards emerged from inside the palazzo, magpies released from their leads and wheeling after her.

'Why are they chasing her?' said Ermin, his dusty face horror-struck.

'I don't know!'

Sofia tried to force her way past the guard again but he held her back, his magpie snapping.

Mamma briefly disappeared, swallowed by the crowd, but then she broke loose, ducking beneath the barriers, and began to run right across the tilted piazza. Ermin gasped.

'What is she *doing*?'

The crowd began to boo, and the woman beside them shuddered.

'She's mad! What if she's sick?'

Her companion shifted, his scarf covering his mouth. 'Could be. Come away.'

'She isn't sick,' hissed Ermin, bouncing nervously on the balls of his feet. 'What's happening?'

Before she could answer, the trumpeter appeared at the palazzo doors. He raised his instrument and tooted three short, deafening blasts.

'Sofia,' said Ermin, his voice shaky with fear. 'What does that mean?'

Sofia couldn't be sure, but the reaction of the crowd confirmed her worst fear.

'They've started the race,' she said faintly. 'He must not have seen her!'

Her imagination showed her awful images. Somewhere, in the corners of the city, the riders would be raising their whips and spurring their horses into action.

'The horses!' she cried, horrified. 'She'll be crushed!'

Mamma was running like a woman possessed. The birds began to swoop, snipping their beaks, pulling at her hair. The crowd jeered. Corvith tried to struggle free of his nest, but Sofia held him in place and passed the skull to Ermin.

'Where are you going?' Ermin gripped on to Sofia's wrist, but Sofia could not think straight. She didn't understand anything of what was happening, but she knew Mamma was in trouble. She had to help her.

Shrugging free of Ermin, heart thrumming in her ears, Sofia forced her way forward and, with the guard distracted by Mamma, slipped under the barrier.

Mamma still had half the piazza to cover and Sofia hurtled towards her, taking the shortest route directly through the centre, panic making her deaf to the shouts of warning rising around her.

Mamma caught sight of her and Sofia saw her expression change, from determined to terrified. Mamma curved towards her, gesturing madly.

'Get back! Go home! The locket—'

Sofia hesitated, her heartbeat filling her whole body, making her legs tremble and seeming to shake the whole ground.

And then Sofia realized. It was not her heart beating that tattoo.

The horses were near.

They burst out on to the piazza like a tidal wave, eyes rolling with effort, their riders like imps crouched on their backs, urging them forward. It was as though time had slowed. Sofia dragged her gaze from the horses back to her mother.

Mamma's eyes were still fixed on Sofia. She had not seemed to notice she was crossing the horses' path and was about to pass the centre point of the piazza, where the swirling black and white seemed to converge like a whirlpool about a drainage grate set into the ground.

Sofia was not going to get to her. Not before—

'Mamma!'

But it was not the horses who reached her first. Two guards had caught Mamma up, and now they snatched her about the waist. They lifted her bodily, magpies screeching, and Mamma kicked and struggled, all the time yelling at Sofia to go, to run.

The whole world was the thunder of horses, and Sofia turned in time to see them bearing down on her. She shut her eyes, as though she might be able to make it all vanish, make everything right if only she could not see what was coming.

Small hands caught her about the waist, forcing her to the ground.

When Sofia opened her eyes, she saw dust and hooves passing close to her head and when she turned to see her rescuer, there was only a glimpse of brown skin.

It was a child, a boy, about her height, his brown eyes intent upon hers. The rest of his face was obscured by a thick scarf. He dragged her clear of the horses and before Sofia could catch her breath, before she could thank him, something in the boy's eyes changed. They narrowed, and then his hand was snatching at her cloak, her neck.

'What the—' Sofia bit and kicked, dust in her eyes, and managed to bite down hard on the boy's hand. He swore loudly and she threw him off in the direction of the horses.

Before Sofia could stop him, before she could do more than shut her eyes again against the horror of it all, he rolled beneath their hooves and was gone, leaving nothing but dust.

6

One moment he was there, the next . . . nowhere.

Sound rushed back to Sofia: screaming, yelling, the trumpeter too late sounding an alarm to stop the race and the crowd surged forwards, overtaking Sofia as she struggled on legs caught in invisible mud.

The horses were rearing, kicking out as the crowd surrounded them, and Sofia could not see Mamma, nor her rescuer-turned-attacker. The guards' magpies were screeching, ducking low over the seething throng, and Sofia felt like she'd fallen into one of the paintings in the cathedral – one full of hellish creatures, and fire, and damnation.

Her breath would not come and even as she tried to fight her way forwards, she felt someone holding her back. Wheeling round, ready to fight her way free from the guard or a well-meaning watcher, she instead saw Ermin's tear-stained face. His eyes were as wide as the horses'.

'Where is Mamma?' he gasped. 'What happened?'

Casting a helpless look at the writhing mass of horses and people, Sofia swallowed her terror, making herself be brave.

'She'll meet us at home. We have to get out of here!'

Sofia swept her little brother into her arms and ran through the twisting, dishevelled streets. More people were pouring towards the piazza, the chaos drawing them like devils. Sofia ran like she was possessed, like Mamma had, and she imagined she had some of her mother's fear in her own chest.

They finally broke out of the narrow streets by the tanning pits, and on to the path home. Sofia, exhausted, lowered Ermin to the ground. She felt dazed, her mouth full of dust. The image of Mamma being dragged away by the guards and the horses bearing down on her filled her mind, repeating like a horrible song.

And the boy, the boy who had saved her life and then grasped for her neck. The boy who she had thrown off, towards the horses . . .

She had not seen him get hit, or trampled, but surely he would not have managed to weave through so many hooves?

'Sofia?' Ermin tugged on her sleeve. 'Are you all right?'

No, she thought. *No, no, no.* It was her fault. Mamma had seen her. That was why she'd run across the centre like that, slowing her down enough for the guards to catch up. It was her fault. She pressed her lips together, against the tide of acrid guilt. Ermin slipped his hand into hers.

'Sofia? Keep going.'

She let him lead her home.

Finally they reached the clean air of their bone-built house and turned the finger-bone key in the knuckle lock. Sofia pulled up a chair to the window, the shutters slightly parted, and peered outside. Ermin climbed into her lap and Corvith settled lightly on her shoulder. His feathery weight was a comfort and he chattered slowly, purring against her ear.

'Mamma will come home soon, won't she?' asked Ermin.

'Yes.' Sofia was not a practised liar, and the word stuck in her throat.

They waited, and waited. The day dropped into a stifling night. The stars hung in a hazy dark sky. Sofia's eyelids grew heavy, her legs aching from sitting on the hard chair. Midnight passed and with it, Sofia's birthday. And they waited on, into the yellow early hours of day again.

Still, though Sofia wished it with every bone of her being, Mamma did not come home.

Sofia was twelve, she told herself sternly, and, more than that, she was a big sister. She knew that however much she wanted to cry, or shout, or panic, she must not, because Ermin and Corvith were relying on her.

So when her brother finally fell asleep, his head lolling on to her shoulder, she swallowed down her tears and lifted him gently, carrying him with great effort to her own bed. It brought back that far-off morning at the well, when Mamma had healed him. Sofia had helped lift him, his body very warm

44

and very light. She tucked him in, echoing Mamma's touch of hand to his forehead. He was blessedly cool. She settled Corvith in his skull nest, stroking his beak until his black eye closed.

Then she took three very deep, very shaky breaths and tried to think. Mamma had promised her a birthday celebration worthy of a saint's day – instead it had turned into a sort of hell. She was so tired from waiting for Mamma to return it felt as though someone had taken up a spoon and stirred her thoughts into a gloopy gruel where nothing would stick. She needed fresh air.

She turned the key very quietly in its lock, the bone bolts smooth and perfect, and went out. It was still early, the day cooler than the one before and scented with lavender from the bushes bunched about the foundations.

She stripped some of the purple herb from its stalks and started to climb the hill, ducking under the dawn-brushed grove. As she walked, she rubbed the flowers between her fingers, recalling Mamma's scent, trying to bring some of her mother's cleverness to her. She broke out from the olive trees, to the well at the top. She drew up water in the bucket, and drank. It was clean and plentiful as always, so why were the wells in the city so low? No wonder everyone was in such a bad temper.

She sighed and sat on the wall of the well. Inlaid on top were their initials: 'R' for Renata, 'S' for Sofia and 'E' for Ermin, all entwined. Mamma had made this little bone emblem for them a few years ago and Sofia had added a wonky 'C' for Corvith when the crow swooped into their lives, an orphan kicked out of his nest.

The bone was worn now, from years of her tracing the intricate letters. This was always her favourite place to think, the place she felt safest and most at home. Across from her, the city was bathed in gold, the white-and-black stripes of the cathedral muted to a burnished shine, the whole city clumped on the hill and seeming small enough to fit in Sofia's pocket. The magpies between the two towers were tiny as flies. At this distance, the cathedral tower was the same size as the one round her neck, and she reached for her locket.

Sofia's heart fluttered in time with the distant magpies' wingbeats.

She checked her neck again, feeling for the clasp. She searched the front of her tunic, down her trouser legs, all the way to her shoes. Then she felt her neck again.

But she was not mistaken. There was no sign of the locket. It was gone.

It matters, Sofia. Keep it safe, always.

Tears welled hot in her eyes, drowning the sight of the distant city, and she was all set to collapse to the ground and wail, when she stopped. The memory of the boy, the one who had saved her from the hooves, floated on the tide of her tears and back into view. His hands, grasping for her neck—

'Thief,' she hissed to the sunrise. 'He's a thief!'

Angrily wiping the tears from her eyes, she set her jaw. She would show him. She would go back to the city and find that boy, and if the horses hadn't got him she would throw him into the nearest well she could find. And if there was no water to cushion his fall, too bad.

Sofia marched back down the hill, new purpose filling her. She'd leave Ermin at home this time, but had better let him know where she was going. She went back inside. But she found the bed sheets pulled back, the room empty.

'Ermin!' She stumbled forward, panic making her clumsy.

The door of the workshop swung open and Sofia turned in time to see her little brother coming out, Corvith in the cranium upon his shoulder, and a pile of assorted bones in his arms.

'Ermin.' Sofia melted with relief. 'What are you doing?'

He carefully lowered the pile of bones into the middle of the floor, where they sat in a pool of golden sunlight that streamed in from the open front door, misty with dust.

'Happy birthday!'

Sofia blinked at him.

'Well, really it's a second birthday.'

'Ermin . . .' Sofia started, as gently as she could. 'Mamma is—'

'Home soon,' he said, a little too fast. 'You said so.'

'I did?'

'Yes,' said Ermin. 'You told me. She'll straighten it out with the guards and come home. So we might as well get on with this in the meantime.'

'Get on with what?'

Ermin grinned. 'The new bone bed, like Mamma said. I've measured it all out, so we can build it bigger.'

Sofia turned back to the door and screwed up her eyes. A moment later she felt Ermin's hand on her shoulder, as high as he could reach.

'Don't you like it? You're always hitting your head, so I thought . . .'

Sofia swallowed down the lump in her throat. 'It's not that.'

'So, you can help me then? I think this is everything we need . . .' He chewed his lip, like he always did when he was upset or nervous. 'I'm sorry. We can wait for Mamma.'

'No, we can't!' Sofia's temper was more at herself, but still she shrugged off his hand. All her resolve to go to the city had melted away, and she felt very tired and alone.

But she wasn't alone. From behind her, there was the soft scrape of bone on bone as Ermin began to gather his gift up. She wasn't being fair. She took another deep breath.

'Wait.' She rubbed her eyes and turned round.

Ermin was straightening with the pile in his arms, his sweet face serious. 'Yes. Please. Let's do it. It's a lovely idea.' She hoisted a weak smile on to her face. 'Let's build the bed bigger.'

7

They opened all the windows to let as much light in as possible and moved the furniture out of the way. Ermin fetched Mamma's tools from the workroom: a wrench, pliers, glue beads from bones they'd boiled themselves, a special hammer that was coated in rubber so it could knock bones together without shattering them, sandpaper made of crushed molars stuck to leather.

'I couldn't find her chisel,' he said, frowning.

'We'll make do,' said Sofia, looking down at the tools: everything they would need to break and then remake the bed.

They lined up the bones in size order, from the femurs that would form the extra length of the frame to the ribs for the struts. They took the sheets off the bed and Sofia carefully removed the canopy of toe bones, placing it safely on the table.

The bed, like all their mother's handiwork, was sturdily made and the legs would not come loose easily. Luckily, Mamma was too skilled to use glue and so it was simply a case of loosening the joins and then everything would slide apart. Still, it took Sofia ten minutes to remove the first leg and a further fifteen for the second. Ermin was the better builder, but pride prevented her from asking him to take over. She whistled Corvith awake from his cranium bed on the desk and got him to measure out enough glue beads in his beak to affix the extra femurs.

Once Corvith had grumpily done this and been rewarded with bread dipped in honey, they let the glue beads melt over a lamp. The room, already hot from the afternoon sun, filled with the heady smell, stinging Sofia's throat – but it was too familiar to be unpleasant. It always sent Corvith to sleep, and she supposed its effects were stronger for birds and other small things.

They sanded down the joint ends of the femurs, until they were straight enough to fit flush with the existing frame. Mamma would have worked out a way to make them all slot together, but this was beyond them. They placed a clamp over the join to help it hold.

'There!' said Sofia, regarding their creation. It didn't look pretty, but it would stay strong. 'Now to hang the canopy.'

Knock knock.

The siblings froze. Sofia held her breath, pressing Ermin to her.

'Who is it?' hissed her brother.

'I can no more see through walls than you,' she whispered back. Her heart was thumping. She hadn't locked the door.

Knock knock knock knock.

Sofia's mind cantered. Mamma would not knock. She stood and approached the rattling door warily. But before she could reach it, there was another knock, harder this time, and the unlocked door flew open.

Ermin screamed.

A giant magpie, high as a man and with a great stabbing beak, stood in the doorway, its black-clawed foot clutching a ball of fire. A massive crow stood beside it.

Sofia stumbled, reaching to slam the door shut,

but as she did so the world resolved into sense again.

It was not a magpie but a palazzo guard, holding a lamp. In his blue-and-white livery and black gloves he was a poor imitation of the bird chained on his shoulder, but the long cone protruding from his face was rather beakish.

Beside him stood not a crow, but a woman in long black robes. A nun.

'Mff mffr mm!' shouted the guard, voice muffled by the cone. Sofia recognized it as a doctor's mask, like the one the man who had come to see Ermin had worn during the smallpox epidemic. She could faintly smell the rosemary and mint it was stuffed with, to purify the air he breathed.

It brought back the memory of the night the doctor had said there was nothing to be done for Ermin. Sofia sniffed her sleeve, scented with lavender, to comfort herself as the man repeated himself. 'Mff mffr mm!'

Sofia's hands were shaking, and she tried to steady them. 'I don't understand.'

'I told him the cone was unnecessary,' sighed the nun. 'Take it off, man.'

The guard lifted his cone warily and repeated himself, parting his lips only slightly.

'This is the house of Signora Fiori?' He was tall and thin, casting nervous glances at the piles of bones as he hovered the mask before him.

Sofia rolled her eyes. Some people were superstitious about their bone house, thinking it held pox and death, when actually the washed bones were the purest, cleanest materials imaginable.

'It is.'

'You are Sofia Fiori?'

'Yes,' said Sofia cautiously. 'Did my mother send you?'

'And this is Ermin Fiori? I am here at the command of the duchessa. You are to come with me.'

Sofia shrank back. Was this the guard who had arrested Mamma, here to arrest them too? The nun tutted, seemingly at the guard's rudeness.

Sofia was regretting not locking the door. 'How do you know our names?'

The guard sighed impatiently. 'I am a duchessa's guard and do not have to explain myself to you.'

'Really,' said the nun sternly. 'I apologize, child. I told him you'd give us no trouble, and that I could come on my own, but apparently the duchessa insisted. She's so precious about her subjects, especially her little ones.'

Sofia wrinkled her nose. *Her* little ones?

'I'm Sister Rosa.' She gave Sofia a warm, kindly smile that stretched her round face like kneaded dough. 'And I'm from the Serafina Convent.'

Sofia's throat filled with acid. The Serafina Convent, named for the duchessa herself. The orphanage. She began to shake her head. Ermin sidled up beside her.

'The convent?'

'Yes, child.' Sister Rosa turned her smile upon him, too. 'We had reports of children living alone. We're here to fetch you.'

'Fetch us?' Ermin looked up at Sofia, but she could not meet his gaze. 'Why?'

'Because of the kindness of the duchessa, who built that place for your sort.'

'We're not orphans,' croaked Sofia. 'Our mamma, she's—'

'Indisposed,' said the nun kindly. 'Yes, dear.'

'But where is she? Why is she—'

'Enough,' said the guard.

'All we know,' said the nun, holding out a placatory hand to him, 'is that a letter came from the palazzo to say two children lived alone in the charnel house and were to be placed under our care.'

'Can't we stay here?'

'You must come with us. The duchessa has ordered it.'

Sofia shook her head. The day was falling away, and dusk would soon settle blue and chill about their home. They could not leave, could not, surely, believe what they were being told and give up on Mamma's return?

'Will we see Mamma?'

'I know nothing but what I was told,' said Sister Rosa softly. 'I will try to find more answers for you. We must go now.'

Something – some bone-deep thing – stayed Sofia. But Ermin was already allowing himself to be manoeuvred inside to fetch his cloak and the guard had crossed his arms sternly. The magpie was eyeing Corvith beadily and though Sofia knew she could wait and wait, there were no more answers here.

She tried to coax Corvith into his cranium basket but the crow hopped from foot to foot, sniping at her with his beak and chittering.

'No–so!'

'I'm sorry,' said Sister Rosa gently. 'We do not allow pets.'

'He's not a pet,' said Ermin. 'He's family.'

'Surely he will be all right here?' said Sister Rosa. 'Crows are made to be free anyway, not caged in a bone house.'

'He's lived with us always,' said Sofia, her heart wrenching at the thought of leaving him. 'He has to come.'

But as she wrestled Corvith into his skull nest the guard's magpie darted at him and was pulled back by its lead, its beak snipping the air. Corvith screeched and took off from Sofia's hands, swooping out of the door and past the guard, disappearing into the twisting shadows of the overgrown olive grove.

'Corvith!' Ermin went stumbling after him, but it was too late. The crow had vanished into the dark, black feathers melting into black air.

★

The stars were bright and white in their places, the moon a precise slice in the inscrutable fabric of the sky. The city felt transformed, or perhaps it was only Sofia's heart that was hollow and haunted.

She was weak with tiredness and could barely walk as the nun and the guard led them through the streets to the richer district of the city, where merchants lived.

'The duchessa ensured the convent was in the finest district,' chattered the nun. 'Built over the spot of the original well to the hidden river. And she used the finest building materials to make it.'

Sofia heard her as though through water. Ermin walked in a daze beside her, yawning with tiredness. They arrived at the convent gates and Sofia could see that it was a beautiful building, built in the same ornate style as the palazzo. There were pipes here too, the kind the duchessa used to speak to them at the Palio. The guard opened the massive cross-hatching of metal to a gatehouse. Sofia felt like a fly, drawn into a silken web.

'That'll be all,' said Sister Rosa to the guard, slamming the gate in his face.

Dumbly, they followed the nun out from the gatehouse and into a wide circular courtyard, illuminated by lamps and surrounded by a loop of buildings with high shuttered windows. In the dirt was evidence of play: a hoop and stick, a ball of rags, a scuffed hopscotch grid drawn into the dust. A well was sunk into the centre. But the whole place was silent and ghostly – the only movement was shadowy magpies flying occasionally overhead, guarding the courtyard.

'For our safety,' said Sister Rosa, indicating the birds. 'The duchessa takes great care of the children in her charge.'

Sofia narrowed her eyes at the flying shadows. It felt more like a prison than a convent.

They entered a door across the yard and walked along a corridor with rows of doors on the left. It still smelt new, like forests and the metallic tang of stone dust.

At last Sofia saw more black-clad figures, more nuns like their guide, though none were so friendly-seeming as Sister Rosa. They barely had a glance to spare for the new arrivals, moving in a strangely regimented way as though set on tracks. Ermin was looking around in bewilderment.

Sofia felt she was dreaming.

Dreaming as Sister Rosa gently unfurled their fingers and placed into them sets of coarse linen tunics and trousers. Dreaming as the nun led them down a scrubbed corridor, into another scrubbed corridor and on and on until they reached a wooden staircase. They were ushered up, and, as in a dream, the corridor they were faced with was an exact mimic of the last.

'You can stay here together, tonight,' said Sister Rosa, gesturing to the room. 'I do not wish to disturb the others. But from tomorrow you'll sleep separately, in the boys' and girls' quarters. Here, drink this.'

She pressed two cups to them, and Sofia drank because it was something to do. Milk, laced with something sweet. Honey? It didn't taste like Mamma's, made with lavender.

'Is that better?' Sister Rosa was looking at them kindly. 'I know you are sad. But you have a home here, and a family. You are not alone.'

The nun gave them a last, kind smile and left the

room, leaving them with a single candle. Sofia's head swam. Her eyes were raw from tiredness. Her neck felt bare and vulnerable without her locket, without the comfort of having the gift Mamma made with her. Too late, she wished she had brought something from home. She helped Ermin change into his linen outfit. At last they lay down and sank fast into sleep.

8

'Wake up, children.'

Sofia opened her eyes. It was light, the day leaking in through the slats of the shutters. The voice came again and she sat up, rubbing her eyes. Ermin was beside her, but there was no one else in the room. Where had it come from?

'Corvith!' Ermin reared up as though jabbed. 'Sofia, we left Corvith. What'll we do?'

Her head felt full of clouds. She preferred that, knowing sharper pain lay beneath. She struggled upright. Her new clothes itched, stiff with starch. 'He'll be all right, Ermin. We won't be staying here.'

'We won't?'

'They can't make us—'

'What's that, child?'

Ermin and Sofia jumped. Sister Rosa had

materialized in the doorway, sudden and silent as a thought.

'Nothing,' mumbled Sofia.

'I'm glad you heard me all right.' Sister Rosa gestured to the walls. Along them was nailed a circular rail, with holes at regular intervals. 'It's a new system we are testing. Just like at the palazzo—'

'Pipes!' said Ermin. 'We know, we heard her use them at the—'

Sofia elbowed him. She didn't want them to get in trouble for being at the Palio.

A faint frown flickered across Sister Rosa's face, like a cold breeze guttering a candle. 'I'm here to show you round. Get dressed, and come along.'

They got ready quietly and quickly, then followed the nun from the room.

'This is the new wing.' She gestured at the room they were leaving behind. 'The duchessa is committed to leaving no needy child uncared for.'

Now Sofia was fully awake, she could hear sounds from outside: children laughing and shouting. She peered through one of the shuttered windows and saw the yard was scattered thinly with children playing around the well. There weren't very many of them, and Sofia supposed this was a good thing, meaning that not a lot of children had lost their families to the smallpox.

'It's free time now,' said Sister Rosa over her shoulder, already far ahead with Ermin at her heels and rounding one of the corners. 'An hour in the morning before lessons, an hour after *riposo* — resting time — and an hour in the evening.'

Sofia tried to lock the information into her head. 'Lessons?'

'You'll do sewing,' said Sister Rosa, 'and this is where you sleep.'

They'd arrived at a wing that mirrored where Sofia and Ermin had slept. The beds here were neatly made, with scant signs of disorder — a comb here, a rag doll there.

'What about me?' said Ermin.

'Boys are further along the corridor.' The nun gestured ahead, where a doorway stood open. 'The door between the boys' and girls' rooms is locked at night. And you'll have separate lessons too.'

'Why?'

'Because boys don't sew, child,' said Sister Rosa.

Sofia thought she caught an edge of something in her voice, something like anger. 'You'll learn woodwork, the use of tools.'

'I sew,' said Ermin proudly. 'And my mamma works with tools.'

'Did she?' Sister Rosa sounded genuinely interested.

'She *does*,' corrected Ermin. 'She's a bone—'

'Ermin,' said Sofia sharply.

'That's nice, child.' Sister Rosa hoisted another benign smile on her face. 'Tell me more about your mother?'

But Ermin looked quickly at Sofia, who shook her head.

'Her work seems fascinating,' continued Sister Rosa. 'And that house! How in heaven did she make such a thing?'

Sofia pressed her lips together and scuffed her feet. Sister Rosa's gentle smile hardened for a moment, before she shrugged.

'This way.'

She led them back to the entrance to the girls' quarters and down the staircase they had taken the previous day. As she descended, Sister Rosa turned briefly to look back at Sofia. She was still smiling. A finger of something like fear traced up Sofia's spine.

'These are the boys' lesson rooms,' said the nun once they reached the ground floor, opening another door. Sofia and Ermin peered inside. It smelt of sawdust and bone glue, like home. There were tools ranged along the walls, outlined in ink so it would be noticed if anything was out of place.

'And these are the girls',' Sister Rosa called from further down the corridor. Sofia wrinkled her nose. A font was set next to the entrance, and the room smelt of roses and was furnished with padded benches. It was a very dull room compared to the boys'.

'What if we want to build things?' said Sofia.

'This,' continued Sister Rosa, as if Sofia had not spoken, 'is the portrait of Duchessa Serafina Machelli, for whom the convent is named.'

She gestured at a large portrait hanging between the two workrooms. An exquisite, green-eyed woman stared out at them – her blonde hair caught beneath a coronet, her skin smooth and perfect. In her arms she held a miniature tower, like the one connected to the palazzo, and a magpie was perched on her shoulder. It was looking at the woman with an expression a lot like Sister Rosa's own: admiration and awe.

'She's beautiful,' breathed Ermin, gaping up at the woman.

'She was,' said Sister Rosa.

'She's dead?' Ermin frowned, sounding confused.

'Goodness no, child. Only she keeps to her own company, now. The pipes are all we hear of our leader.' Sister Rosa crossed herself. A sound threw itself through Sofia's body, rippling through the soles of her feet.

Ermin cringed and covered his ears. 'What's that?'

'The bell,' said Sister Rosa, pointing again to the wall. There, high up, was another pipe. 'Come come, lesson time.'

She pointed Sofia to the room in front of them and went to usher Ermin away. Her little brother clung to her.

'I want to stay with Sofia.'

'It's not allowed,' said Sister Rosa, and for the first time something like disapproval crossed her round face.

Sofia didn't want Ermin to leave any more than he wanted to part from her, but she saw there was no arguing with Sister Rosa. She knelt down and hugged Ermin close.

'It's not for long, and you're only next door.' She whispered into his ear. 'I'll figure this out, Ermin. I just need time to think.'

He nodded, lip wobbling, and let Sister Rosa lead him away just as the sound of several pairs of feet slapping on wooden floors reached Sofia. She shrank back against the wall beside the font as a trickle of girls seeped along the corridor.

All wore the same clothes as her and all had their hair in tight plaits that trailed down their backs, tied neatly with rope. Each stopped at the small font outside the room, washing their hands with soap on a rope beside it. They took great care, and Sofia saw some of them counting to ten as they washed.

As they passed Sofia to enter the room they stared openly, whispering behind their hands, and Sofia felt her cheeks colour. She tried to tidy her own hair, wild with tangles, wishing she could disappear into the cool wall behind her.

Sister Rosa brought up the rear and gave Sofia another kind smile as she detached her gently but firmly from her hiding place. She had a knot of string in her hands, and she turned Sofia round to the font.

'Wash your hands.' As Sofia did so, Sister Rosa began yanking her hair into a plait with surprising forcefulness. Sofia winced, but did not draw away.

Once her hands were washed and her hair was secured, Sister Rosa nodded approvingly. 'Much better. Come and meet your new friends.'

9

The girls slotted neatly on to the benches lining the walls, like books into bookshelves, bringing out an assortment of tunics, socks and nightcaps from boxes beneath them.

Sister Rosa clapped her hands once and the rustling and whispering stopped.

'This is Sofia Fiori, girls. Please make her welcome.' The nun gestured for Sofia to sit at the end of the bench. 'You can help Carmela with her darning.'

Sofia turned uncertainly to Carmela. She was a thin girl with a narrow face. She had curled her legs up underneath herself, putting Sofia in mind of a dormouse. Carmela smiled toothily.

'This pillowcase is full of holes,' she whispered. 'I'm glad I have help.'

'Shhh.' Sister Rosa held her finger to her lips. 'Work in silence girls, the better to concentrate.'

Sofia took the needle and thread Carmela offered her and, nodding gratefully, began to work on the frayed pillowcase.

Sofia was not a skilled seamstress. Ermin was the one with delicate fingers, the one Mamma chose to darn their own pillowcases or filigree her bone boxes. Sofia longed to be next door with the boys, a hammer in her hands, making something solid. Work that would make her arms ache, like building the bone bed.

This was boring, but at least it gave Sofia time to think. Only the day before they had been at home. Now they were in an orphanage – and Corvith was at home on his own, and Mamma was arrested, possibly imprisoned – perhaps for ever . . .

No, Sofia told herself firmly. She would not believe it. This was all a big misunderstanding. Mamma would return home soon enough and Corvith would guide her to town, and soon they would be back in their charnel house.

She concentrated more on these thoughts than her work, and Carmela's smile soon dropped when she saw the state Sofia was making of her pillow-case. But still, she was kind, and as the two hours dragged by she gently guided Sofia in her needle-work, so that when that awful bell crashed through the pipe lining the room and into Sofia's body again, her efforts were a little improved.

The girls stretched and packed away their work beneath the benches and stood, Sofia rising a beat after the rest.

'Very good, girls,' said Sister Rosa, who had sat so silently and still that Sofia had almost forgotten she was there. A bell was in her hand. Beside her was a box, with a lever which she now slid to a different position. The echo of the bell faded away. 'Lunch.'

Sofia was swept along in the soft chatter of the girls, swaddled tight to Carmela's side by the crush as they moved along the corridor, beneath the portrait of Duchessa Machelli, past the boys' workroom and into the yard. Tables had been set up with benches beside them, and the watery smell of stew wafted to Sofia.

It was not yet the hottest time of the day, but still Sofia's eyes stung in the sunlight. Magpies endlessly wheeled the perimeter, blots against the dazzling blue.

Sofia was unused to their presence, and to such a limited view. From the olive grove outside their house they could see all of Siena, perched on its neighbouring hills – the summit of the cathedral tower like the arm of a sundial, casting shadows with the other towers of the city as the sun rose and fell.

Here, she felt she could have been anywhere in the world beneath that blue sky. The city might have slipped apart outside, and she would never know it but for those magpies.

The boys were already seated and Sofia found her brother easily, for he was the smallest there, a dip topped with curls in the line of backs. When he turned, she waved and Carmela caught her hand.

'Careful,' she murmured. 'They don't like us talking to the boys.'

'He's my brother,' hissed Sofia.

Carmela shrugged. 'I don't make the rules.'

'Who does?'

But Carmela only held a finger to her lips.

Sister Rosa took up her place at the head of the

queue, surveying the scene from beside another nun who ladled out bean stew into rough wooden bowls with brisk efficiency.

Sofia ducked her head when she approached and did not look up until she was safely seated. She reached for her spoon, but again Carmela stayed her hand.

'Let us pray,' said Sister Rosa, and only after the *Amen* were they allowed to eat.

They ate in silence, heads dipping almost in unison. It felt more like an army than a group of orphans. Sofia finished ahead of the other girls on her table and again sought out Ermin.

He was seated facing away from her, but she fixed the back of his neck in such a stare he scratched his nape and turned round. She gave him a brief grin, and he grinned back. The tightness in her chest loosened a notch.

'Listen, children,' said Sister Rosa, her voice soft. 'I know you heard the trumpet signalling the Palio yesterday. What you may not know was that there was an incident . . .' The nun paused and looked pitifully at Sofia. She felt a trickle of sweat race down her collarbone. 'The duchessa has rescheduled the

Palio for two days' time. Just in case you wonder about the trumpet sounding again.'

A sigh of longing rippled round the courtyard.

'The Palio,' murmured Carmela. 'I've never seen it, or the duchessa!'

'How long have you been here?' frowned Sofia.

'Three years,' said Carmela. 'Since the smallpox.' She whispered the word, like the disease were a harpy that would swoop down and carry her away if it heard her.

'And the duchessa has not visited? I thought it was her orphanage?'

'Sister Rosa runs it really. The duchessa is in mourning, she doesn't leave the palazzo – everyone knows it. But if only we were allowed to go to the Palio, just think who might see us!'

'Why would that matter?' asked Sofia.

'Someone might wish to adopt us,' said Carmela wistfully. 'Though sometimes we are adopted without meeting our new parents. There was a girl, Artie. She got adopted only last week – it happened overnight. We were all so surprised. She'd been sick you see, but then one night she was just gone! Isn't it marvellous?'

It sounded strange to Sofia, and offered another danger she had not considered. What if someone saw − not her, for she could look fierce if she needed to − but Ermin? With his sweet face and soft curls, he would be a treasure. She eyed him, considering. She would have to dirty his face. Not that they would stay here for long.

With the bowls empty, they were passed down to the end of each row and carried inside. Ermin was at the end of his row, and the boys' bowls teetered in his hands. Carmela was just about to lift her own crockery tower when Sofia caught hold of her sleeve.

'I'll take them.'

'It's just inside to the right. You'll have to wash up, too.'

'I don't mind.'

Carmela handed them over and went back to excitedly discussing the Palio with her friends.

Sofia followed Ermin into the shadowy corridor. He was already well ahead of her, concentrating on the balancing bowls.

'Ermin, slow down.'

She hurried to catch him just as he pulled up

and she collided with him, sending bowls and spoons flying down the corridor.

'Ermin!' chided Sofia, as though it were not half her fault.

'I didn't—'

Sofia cut him off, holding up her hand. 'Go and put those in the sink. I'll tidy these.'

She grubbed around on her hands and knees, scooping up bowls with bad grace. At least none of the nuns had been there to see her make a mess. She stacked the bowls beside a closed door, trying to avoid the small pools of leftover stew dotted about. She sighed. She would have to wipe the corridor before the nuns saw.

Reaching for a final bowl, Sofia heard a quiet creak behind her. She froze, expecting a nun's sharp voice, but none came. The creak came again, a little louder this time, and Sofia wheeled round.

At first, she saw nothing. The corridor was empty. Then, a tiny movement, like a moth, snagged on her vision. It made so little sense that at first her brain tried to dismiss it.

The door beside the stack of bowls was open just a fraction and Sofia could see a slice of a large cupboard, lined with shelves. Through the gap, came a hand. A dark, nimble hand, with bite marks circling the thumb.

10

As Sofia watched, too shocked to move, the bitten hand lifted a bowl from the stacked pile, together with a spoon, and withdrew back into the shadows of the barely opened door.

It was so quick, she would have missed it had she blinked. But now Sofia's surprise melted away, and before the door could be pushed closed she scrambled forwards and stuck her own fingers into the gap.

'Ouch!'

The door squeezed them painfully, and from inside the cupboard came a small gasp of surprise. Emboldened by the fact she had caught the thief unawares, Sofia placed her shoulder to the wood and shoved.

She tumbled forwards, directly on top of the writhing figure.

'Let go!'

She saw his face bundled up in a scarf and his dark brown eyes, before the boy from the Palio kicked the door closed, plunging them into semi-darkness.

'You!'

'Let go,' said the boy, panting. Sofia tightened her grip. 'You're hurting me.'

'Good,' snarled Sofia. 'Give me back my locket.'

'What?' The boy wriggled, but Sofia was made strong by fury.

'My locket! The locket you stole from me. At the Palio.'

'I didn't – ouch!' Sofia had dug her fingers into his bruised hand. 'Fine! Fine. You can have it.'

She loosened her grip. 'Come on then.'

'I don't have it with me.' He danced away from Sofia's grip. 'I'll get it!'

She looked around them at the gloom of the cupboard. 'What are you doing in here?'

'None of your business.'

'Why did you take my locket?'

'It just fell off.'

Sofia knew Mamma's clasp would never fail like that.

'But you were grabbing me.' The boy stared at her impassively. Sofia ground her teeth. 'Well go on then, get it.'

'I will.'

She stood up. In the cramped space she had to be careful not to hit her head on a shelf. 'You coming?'

The boy didn't answer. Sofia *hurrumphed* and let herself out of the cupboard. The door slammed shut behind her.

'Rude,' she muttered, tapping her foot and waiting for him to emerge. She would tell Sister Rosa that one of her orphans was stealing bowls, hiding out in cupboards. She would tell the nun she'd seen him at the Palio.

Ermin poked his head round the door to the kitchen. 'I need your help.'

Sofia bent to pick up the bowls, but her anger bubbled up again. There really was no call for the boy being so rude to her when he was the thief here. She opened the door again, ready to give him a piece of her mind.

'Sofia?' Ermin sounded impatient. 'I can't reach the soap.'

But Sofia could not answer him. For the second time in as many minutes, she was struck dumb.

The cupboard was empty.

Sofia's mind churned as Ermin gabbled about his class.

'We were making joins,' said Ermin proudly. 'And I made the best ones. Father Retto says I'm a born carpenter.'

'I don't care about the lessons,' said Sofia huffily. 'Ermin, listen.'

She told him about the locket, the boy, his disappearing act from the cupboard. Once they had dried up, she took him and showed him. It was still empty.

'Are you sure he didn't just hide behind the door?'

'There's no room.'

'Well,' said Ermin slowly, and Sofia could tell he didn't wholly believe her. 'He's not there now.'

'Yes,' snapped Sofia. 'I can see that.'

'Mamma told you to keep that locket safe.'

'Yes, I know that too!'

'There you are.' Sister Rosa was standing behind

them. She moved quiet as a mouse. Her eyes bore into them. Sofia didn't know if she was being paranoid, but it felt like Sister Rosa stared at them more intently than at the other children. Perhaps Sofia would wait to tell her about the boy in the cupboard. 'Time for *riposo*.'

The children began to file inside, and Sister Rosa ushered Ermin into the boys' line, gesturing for Sofia to join the girls' line.

Sofia's heart was still galloping, and though she joined the queue and filed obediently out under the watchful gaze of the Sisters, washing her dusty feet with a cloth and slipping into the clean, musty sheets for the afternoon nap, she knew she would not be able to sleep.

Sofia was not alone in her restlessness. But the other girls were abuzz with excitement, not confusion. All their whispered talk was of the Palio, and the possibility of finding a family.

'Do you think Sister Rosa will let us wear different clothes if we're allowed to go?' whispered Carmela.

'I doubt it,' said a tall girl called Lucia. 'But we could brush out our hair and leave it down.'

'Artie had nice hair,' said Carmela, nodding. 'Do you think that's why she was chosen?'

'But Guilia didn't,' said Lucia thoughtfully. 'And she was the first one. Nor Laura, or Stella.'

'And boys never have nice hair,' said a stubby-nosed girl called Flavia. 'And some of them got chosen, didn't they?'

'Who chose them?' asked Sofia.

'We don't know,' said Carmela longingly. 'They went overnight. They didn't even say goodbye. I would have thought at least Maria would have come back to visit.'

'I wouldn't come back,' said Flavia decidedly. 'Sorry, but if I get chosen, I'm never setting foot in here again.'

'*When*,' corrected Carmela. 'When you get chosen.' She beamed round at them. 'We all will, I can feel it.'

Sofia ducked her head. She already had a family and held no desire for some rich woman to come in the night and take her away. She needed to get herself and Ermin out of here, and fast. She thought then of the mysterious boy, how he seemed able to come and go. 'Do people ever just . . .' She paused, wondering how to put it. 'Vanish?'

'Escape, you mean?' Lucia sounded scandalized. 'Life's no better out there than in here. There's no water, and people are still poor from the pox. The duchessa looks after us.'

'Was there a boy, who left? Or maybe he hasn't. He looks . . .' But Sofia wasn't sure how he looked. His face had been covered each time. She flapped her hand. 'He has brown eyes.'

Carmela wrinkled her nose. 'So do lots of people.'

'He hides his face.' She looked from Carmela to Flavia. 'He was in the big cupboard by the kitchen. You've not seen him?'

Flavia was eyeing Sofia warily. 'Sounds like you're imagining things.'

Sofia knew she was not imagining him. The boy had saved her from the horses and stolen her locket. She had bitten his hand and wrestled him in the cupboard. But where had he gone?

Sofia had never felt more powerless in all her life. Mamma had brought her up to believe she and Ermin could achieve anything they set their minds to, but here in the orphanage she was learning that children were seen as a thing apart. More than that, girls were seen as less capable than boys and trusted only with the soft work of cloth and thread. She missed Ermin, missed Corvith and, most of all, longed for Mamma. Mamma would know what to do.

Sister Rosa arrived to wake them and they filed out under her watchful gaze. The nun's fixed smile now decidedly gave Sofia the creeps.

They were ushered back down the stairs, into the ground-floor corridor, but this time to a room at the far edge of the orphanage, the smell of tar soap strong in the air. Piles of clothes were heaped before the wooden vats of water, freshly boiled and steaming, and a furnace like the one at home roared in the corner, making Sofia's scalp prickle with sweat. One pile was muddy with the grey of their uniform, another the black of the nuns' habits.

'This half, those. This half, those.' Sister Rosa smiled again as she divided them down the middle.

Sofia sighed as she realized the boys would not be joining them to help, and moved obediently to the pile of black with Carmela, Lucia and Flavia. They each took up a paddle and looked at Sofia expectantly. She realized that she was to move the dirty clothes into the vats, so they could stir them.

The fabric of the nuns' robes was softer than the children's coarse linen — a fine cotton that was as buttery as Sofia's bed sheets at home. Sofia could only manage a couple at a time, so voluminous was the material. It was slow work, lifting and then waiting for the cloth to be washed, then placing it through the wringer. This was the hardest job and, again, was left to Sofia as the new girl.

Her arms ached as they reached the bottom of the pile. The wringer's handle was stiff and chafed her palms. They never used one at home, letting clothes dry in the sun — spread across the branches of the olive trees, lavender stuffed in pockets so they were filled with their scent. A wave of homesickness punched at Sofia's gut, but a moment later she saw something that made her throat close with fear.

A shadowy figure, shooting beneath her, past a vent in the floor.

Her fingers stumbled on the wringer's handle and she let the robes drop with a wet slap to the floor. As she watched, the vent opened a crack and that same, bitten hand slipped out, snatching a white washcloth.

'Tut, tut,' said Sister Rosa merrily, sweeping over to her. 'These will have to be rewashed—'

The nun stopped short as she reached Sofia, and her smile dropped. She cast a sharp glance from the vent, to the girls clustered round the vats. They were talking and laughing softly as they stirred, intent on their work and each other.

'This is ruined, child.' Sister Rosa turned back to Sofia, that fixed smile back on her face and her voice so sweet it made Sofia's teeth ache. 'You must learn when to pay more attention. And when to pay less.'

11

Sofia felt the nun's eyes on her as she guided them back into the yard for their hour of evening play. Sister Rosa knew what Sofia had seen under the floor, she was sure of it.

Did Sister Rosa know about the boy's presence? And, if she did, why did she allow it? If he was simply a thief, she should get him removed. But what if there was more to it? Something strange was happening here – and Sofia was convinced it was something bad. She had to get Ermin away from the orphanage as soon as possible.

Her brother was amongst the last of the boys to emerge from their workshop into the yard. She could tell from the sawdust on his cheek they had been building things again.

Several of the boys were throwing themselves

into the dirt after the ball of rags, and Sofia gritted her teeth. They were thoughtless with their clothes because they didn't have to wash them whereas the girls were careful, knowing it would be them hunched in that hot, horrid room getting out stains.

'We made hinges, Sofia,' chattered Ermin, running up to her. 'And the teacher says mine are the finest—'

'We have to go,' hissed Sofia, gripping him tightly.

'But we don't have permission—'

'Without permission.' She was looking round, but Sister Rosa was nowhere to be seen. 'Now.'

'I . . .'

'What?'

'I don't . . . I think I want to stay here, Sofia.' Spotting the rage on her face, he hurried on. 'Just for a little bit. If Mamma really is going to be gone a while—'

'Don't say that,' said Sofia harshly.

'But we're looked after here. We're fed and our clothes are cleaned—'

'*We* clean your clothes, you dolt. The girls.'

'Well,' said Ermin mulishly, jutting out his chin. 'I quite like it here.'

'Only because you're the teacher's pet,' said Sofia meanly. 'Only because you like the attention.'

'Sofia, I—'

'And you've given up on Mamma already. We only have that nun's word about what happened to her, and I don't trust her. I think she knows about the boy I saw earlier—'

'Are you sure you saw him?'

'—and something strange is going on. We have to go, and we have to go tonight.'

'Corvith,' said Ermin suddenly.

'Exactly. Corvith needs us and—'

'No, Corvith!' Ermin was pointing now, and Sofia glanced up as a muffled caw came from above them. A boy nearby gasped at the sky.

'Those magpies, they're fighting!'

Sofia shielded her eyes from the low afternoon sun. She did not immediately spot the two shapes silhouetted against the glare but when she did, she cried out too.

Like Ermin, Sofia knew it was not two magpies. She would recognize Corvith anywhere. Their crow had found them, but he had also found trouble.

'No, no, no!'

A magpie was pecking and diving at Corvith. A black feather was pulled from Corvith's wing and he let out a squawk of pain that made her heart ache.

'He's hurting him!' Tears sprang into Sofia's eyes. She felt completely helpless.

Corvith began to fall, his wing crumpling. Ermin rushed forwards, holding out his arms. Corvith landed in them with a soft *thump* and cawed pitifully. Sofia hurried towards Ermin, glancing round to check if the nuns had seen, but the yard was unsupervised.

'Eurgh,' said Flavia, wrinkling her nose. 'Don't touch it.'

'Sister Rosa will never let you take that bird inside,' said Carmela, a little more kindly. 'You'll have to hide it.'

Sofia stroked Corvith with her thumb, thinking hard. There was no way of smuggling Corvith to their dormitory in their pocketless tunics and he was obviously in no condition to fly, though thankfully his injuries did not seem too serious. She could see a little blood but he let her stroke his wing gently, which meant it was likely not broken.

'Sofia?' Ermin's voice trembled and she squeezed his arm, their fight forgotten. 'What shall we do?'

Casting another quick glance round the yard, Sofia pulled him wordlessly back inside to the cupboard where the boy had been hiding earlier. It was still unlocked. She took a bowl from the shelf, and tore off some fabric from the hem of her tunic to make Corvith a little nest.

'Here,' she said, taking the crow from Ermin's arms and placing him gently down. 'We'll come back for him.'

'Tonight?'

'As soon as the others are asleep.' She smiled in what she hoped was a reassuring manner, but she felt her lip wobble. It had been awful seeing Corvith attacked like that.

Ermin nodded, stroking the crow before Sofia lifted him up to a high shelf so that he would not be easily spotted.

'You'll be all right, Corvith. Stay quiet, all right?'

'So-so!' said the bird mournfully.

They slipped from the cupboard and made it to the yard just before the pipes rattled with Sister Rosa's voice.

'Dinner time, children.'

12

Once they were fed and tucked up in bed, each of them was given a cup of milk and honey just as Sofia and Ermin had received the previous night. It smelt like heaven. How many times had Mamma made this for them, her clever hands working quick and light? The morning of Sofia's birthday felt an age ago.

Carmela and most of the others drank as soon as possible, burning their tongues and sighing, and Sofia felt a rush of sadness. Not for herself but for these children who were so excited for their milk and honey, who perhaps could not even remember their mothers placing a warm cup into their hands.

'Here,' she said and held out her cup to Carmela.

'What?' The girl blinked at her, surprised.

'You can have it.'

Carmela slipped from her bed and slid in beside Sofia, still looking uncertain. 'Are you sure?'

Sofia shifted to make more room and closed Carmela's fingers round the cup. 'I'm sure.'

'That's really kind.'

'Thanks for being nice to me,' said Sofia. 'At sewing. I'm sorry about ruining the pillowcase. I was tired.'

Carmela nodded and squeezed Sofia's fingers lightly. 'I was too, when I arrived.'

It was with a slightly lighter heart that Sofia watched Carmela drain the second cup. Within an hour or two she would see Corvith and talk to Ermin. Then she would work out how to get them all home. The only thorn stinging her side was that boy, and how to get her locket back. But that was a problem for another day. In the meantime, she would become better friends with Carmela.

Carmela didn't return to her own bed – she was already asleep, her head lolling on to her shoulder. Sofia prodded her lightly, but the girl was softly snoring. Frowning, Sofia climbed carefully out of her bed and into Carmela's, looking round to see if anyone had noticed what just happened.

But the other girls were asleep, too. So Sofia lay down under Carmela's sheets and wondered how long she should wait before sneaking out. At home, she never had to know what the time was — she always knew where her brother and mother were and what they were doing.

No, said a small voice in her head. *Not always*. What had happened to Mamma? Why she had been so sad and why she had been arrested was another mystery Sofia felt needling under her skin like a splinter. She rubbed her hand roughly over her face, trying to wipe away the vision of Mamma being dragged away from the piazza.

Sofia rolled on to her side, impatient for time to pass. Her eyes had adjusted to the gloom and she could see that in the bed next to her, Carmela's eyes were shut and she was breathing deep and slow.

The door creaked open. Sofia caught sight of someone in the doorway. Sister Rosa. Sofia lay very still. The figure seemed to stand there for a long time.

Eventually, Sister Rosa stepped aside and pointed. A guard and his magpie passed her, creeping into the room.

Sofia heard the floorboards creak near her bed and tried to slow her breathing. Was the guard checking each of them individually? She chanced a quick glance. The man was leaning over Carmela. He pointed at the bed and Sister Rosa nodded. The guard prodded the girl's cheek: Carmela did not stir.

Sofia watched through half-open lids as he placed a sack over Carmela's head and lifted the girl from her bed. Sofia wanted to scream, but her voice was trapped in her throat. She must have made some noise because the guard turned so quickly, Carmela slung over his shoulder, that Sofia only just closed her eyes in time before she felt him loom above her. The magpie on his shoulder chattered softly.

Sofia rolled over as if still asleep and only a little disturbed, keeping her eyes firmly shut. Her heart thudded, the sound so loud in her ears it was like a bell clanging through the orphanage pipes.

But the presence moved away. There was a scraping sound before the door closed, and the room was plunged once more into darkness.

Sofia leapt to her feet, staring in horror at the empty sheets on her bed. None of the other girls stirred. Sofia checked the other beds. All were sleeping soundly – too soundly. Her stomach roiled as she thought of Ermin. What if he had been taken?

She slipped on her shoes and opened the door a crack. The corridor looked, and sounded, deserted. She slipped out and crept along it, keeping to the edges to stop the more worn boards at the centre from creaking.

When she reached the top of the stairs, she listened. She heard a scraping sound and the grating of a gate. She moved quickly to the window at the end of the passage, just in time to see the sack-covered Carmela loaded on to a low cart. Sister Rosa swung herself up beside the cart driver and as she did so, Sofia saw the outline of breeches beneath her habit. Did nuns usually wear a uniform under their robes?

The horse was whipped into action and soon vanished into the darkness of the street.

Sofia's heart was thunderous. She waited a little longer.

Silence.

She inched down the stairs. The ground-floor corridor was empty. Moving towards the cupboard as though in a dream, everything feeling unreal in the faint moonlight, she hurried inside.

'Sofia!' Ermin's panicked voice came fast and low.

'Shhh!' chided Sofia, relief flooding her body. 'Ermin, quiet. There's someone else up, someone taking children—'

'Sofia,' said Ermin, louder than before. 'Corvith's gone!'

Sofia's relief turned to ice. She felt along the highest shelf in the pitch black, searching for the bowl containing the precious crow. But when she found it, it held nothing but the fabric from her tunic.

Her head spun. 'He can't be – there's no way . . .'

A grinding sound came through the dark. Ermin clutched her. 'What was that?'

The sound came again, like the scraping sound she had heard earlier – but closer. It was coming from inside the cupboard. No – she listened harder. The sound was coming from *behind* the cupboard. From a solid wall.

'Sofia . . .'

She heard Ermin scrabbling for the door handle, but before he found it there was a final, high-pitched grating sound that set her teeth on edge. Cold air, as sudden as a wave, crashed into her, sucking at her hair and tunic. Light rushed in with it: an orange, wavering light.

An amused voice emerged from the shadows. 'Hello.'

13

A lamp was thrust into the space between Sofia and Ermin. And, illuminated in its light, was the half-hidden face of the thief.

'How—'

'Shhh!' The thief reached out and clasped Sofia's wrist. 'This way.'

'What are you doing?'

'You're making a racket,' chided the boy.

'Where's Corvith?'

'The crow? He was making a racket, too, so I moved him. Follow me.'

And he stepped, not through the wall, but into it. By the lamp's glow Sofia could see that part of the back wall of the cupboard was missing, the edges clean and the space beyond it dark and smelling of earth.

The boy turned back to look at them. 'Come on, your crow's waiting.'

Ermin needed no further encouragement. He followed the boy through the hole. Sofia leant forward. There was a slope leading down, away from the cupboard.

Sofia lowered herself carefully into the tunnel, which was big enough to stand in. Her knees jarred painfully as she tried to control her pace. The boy made his way back up the slope and lifted the section of wall back into place, covering the hole they had just passed through.

'What is this?'

'A tunnel,' said the boy unhelpfully. 'Quickly.'

Sofia followed, gripping on to Ermin's shoulder, round a shallow bend.

'Here we are.'

'Corvith!' Ermin hurried forward. The crow was settled in his bowl in the centre of the tunnel. Beneath him was a white cloth, and Sofia recognized it as the one she'd dropped in the laundry room.

When Corvith saw them, he gave a beleaguered squawk as if to say *what took you so long.*

'I gave him some crumbs and water,' said the

boy. He was standing a little way off, watching them uncertainly. 'He seems all right. Just a bit grumpy.'

'That's normal,' said Ermin.

Sofia lifted the crow into her lap. He seemed much recovered, his wing smooth with no sign of blood.

'You shouldn't have moved him—'

'What she means is, thank you,' interrupted Ermin. 'Thank you for helping him. I'm Ermin.'

'Ghino,' said the boy, holding out his hand for Ermin to shake. He held out his hand to Sofia, too, and she eyed his grimy palm warily.

'This is Sofia,' said Ermin. 'She's not usually so prickly.'

'I'm not being prickly,' said Sofia, in a particularly spiky voice. 'I just don't know why he brought Corvith down here.'

'He was safer here.'

'And where *is* here? And don't –' she glared at Ghino – 'say a tunnel.'

'Well,' said Ghino, leaning on the rough earth wall. 'That is what it is.'

'All right, but why is it here? Why are *you* here?'

'I live here.'

'In the tunnel?' Ermin gawped at him.

'This one, and others. I have the whole place to myself.' He stretched his arms out.

'Doesn't look like much,' said Sofia scathingly.

'That's where you're wrong.' Ghino looked round proudly, like he was the duchessa showing off her palazzo. 'These tunnels, they go under the whole of Siena. It's my very own city.'

'You're an escaped orphan?' Sofia gestured at his tunic, the same as she and Ermin wore.

Something like hurt flashed across Ghino's face.

'Sofia,' hissed Ermin.

'Why are you dressed like that?' Sofia persisted.

'I sometimes borrow things,' said Ghino, looking at her defiantly. 'Clothes, food—'

'Bowls,' snapped Sofia. 'Spoons. *Lockets*.'

'Crockery is rather hard to come by down here.'

'And you give it back?'

'What?'

'You said you borrow things.' She crossed her arms, causing Corvith to grumble and hop on to Ermin's lap instead. 'You return them then?'

'Not so far.'

'So, you're a thief.'

Ghino shrugged. 'They don't notice things go. Though they might realize you're missing.'

'What about your face?' said Sofia. 'Why do you hide it? It makes you look shifty.'

'Sofia!' Ermin said. 'You're being rude.'

The boy glared at her, and she glared back.

'Well?'

'You should get back to bed,' said the boy stonily. 'I can look after Corvith until he's better.'

'We're not going back,' said Sofia, remembering suddenly the more urgent matter of what she had seen. 'I think Sister Rosa is taking children.'

Ermin frowned. 'What do you mean?'

'She takes them at night, takes them . . . somewhere. The girls were saying they get adopted, but I think she steals them.'

'Bit hard to steal a person,' said Ghino, laughing a little too loudly.

'And you'd know all about stealing,' snapped Sofia. 'I think she puts something in the milk.'

'Honey?' said Ermin, confused.

'Something to make them sleep. You didn't drink yours, did you?'

'No, I . . .' He looked at Ghino, as though embarrassed by what he was about to say. 'It made me think of Mamma. I gave it away.'

'So did I,' said Sofia, nodding. 'I gave mine to Carmela and she was taken.'

Sofia told them about Carmela being bundled away by the guard, and the cart at the gates. 'That nun's up to something.'

'I don't know,' said Ghino, shrugging. 'Maybe she got adopted.'

'But it was my bed,' said Sofia.

'Then maybe you were meant to be adopted. You should go back and find out.'

Sofia narrowed her eyes at him. 'Do you think I'm stupid?'

'Clearly,' said Ghino, in such an insufferable tone Sofia's patience snapped.

She lunged at him. She wanted her locket back and perhaps he was wearing it under the scarf, around his neck. She caught him by surprise and he knocked the lamp sideways, sending shadows spurting crazily up the walls.

Corvith squawked indignantly and Ermin shouted at her to stop, but Sofia's hand had already caught in the snarl of cloth and she pulled it loose.

'No!' cried Ghino as the scarf fell to the floor. The locket wasn't round his neck, but now Sofia saw why he kept his face hidden.

Craters, deep enough to put her thumb into, dotted his jaw with scar tissue, matting about his mouth. He was scarred by the pox.

He moaned and snatched his cloth.

'I'm . . . I'm sorry,' stuttered Sofia. 'I just wanted my locket.'

'Here's your stupid locket,' snapped the boy, digging in his pocket while his other hand wrapped the scarf back round his face. He flung it at Sofia. She caught and inspected it. It was un-damaged, and still locked. She reclasped it round her neck, and despite her shame, feeling its light presence against her chest again was a relief.

'You don't need to hide your face,' said Ermin, watching the boy as he righted the lamp. 'It doesn't matter.'

Ghino laughed hollowly, tucking the ends of the cloth into his tunic so only his eyes showed, angry and fearful, over the top. 'Tell that to people up top.'

'I am sorry,' said Sofia. 'The locket. My

mamma made it.'

The boy kicked at the ground. 'Done now.'

'It's not that bad,' said Sofia. 'Really—'

'I don't want to talk about it,' snapped Ghino. 'Did you see where they took the girl?'

'West maybe? I can't be sure. But I don't think we should go back to the orphanage. Is there a way of getting out of the city, beyond the boundary?'

'The tunnels stretch all over. They're old riverbeds, sewers and catacombs. They link pretty much the whole city.'

'But why do you live here?'

'Look at me.' Ghino dropped his gaze. 'I was never meant to be up top.'

'Were you born like that?'

'Ermin!' It was Sofia's turn to be disapproving, but Ghino shook his head.

'It was the pox.'

'I had it too,' said Ermin.

'Really?' Ghino searched Ermin's face. 'You're lucky you weren't scarred. I used to live up top, in a village a few miles away. But my parents . . .' Again that look of pain, fast as breath, flickered on his face. 'Well, when I got sick my brother did too. He was the favourite, I know he was, and . . .' Ghino swallowed. 'He didn't make it. I survived but was scarred so badly, they couldn't look at me. They didn't want the reminder. They called me a curse.'

Sofia felt her face flush and clasped her locket. She felt badly for revealing his face, especially when it brought up such painful memories.

'What happened?' asked Ermin.

'My parents tried to heal me. They brought me here, to Siena. They took me to the cathedral, pressed relics on to my skin – the nail of Saint Peregrine, the hair of Saint Lucia – but nothing worked. I heard them saying they were going to have me locked up, in a hospital. So I ran away. It's better for me here anyway. Who wants parents?'

'Our mamma is wonderful,' said Ermin reverently.

'Well,' said Ghino defiantly. 'I like being alone.'

But he looked miserable, and Sofia suspected he was lonelier than he'd admit.

'Anyway,' he said, seeming to pull himself together, 'outside the boundary you said? We can get there by sunrise. And as we go, you can tell me about your *wonderful* mother. This way.'

14

The tunnel seemed to go on endlessly, unspooling like a dark river. But Sofia barely noticed. Her mind was elsewhere, full of questions.

The nuns would surely come looking for them in the charnel house, but they could set Corvith to watch and hide in the olive grove if anyone came. And they would work out what, if anything, could be done about the taken girls. Perhaps they could get a message to Duchessa Machelli, that Sister Rosa was stealing children. Perhaps, in return, she would release Mamma. But why had the guards taken her prisoner anyway? What had Mamma been doing at the palazzo? The need for answers gnawed at her like tiny burrowing insects.

The tunnels were, as Ghino had said, a mishmash of rough earth, cobbled stone and chambers of bone that Mamma would have loved to see. More paths twisted off from the one they took, but Ghino seemed sure of himself. He marked the walls with a chip of chalk as they went, and Sofia knew they had no choice but to trust him.

As they passed through a catacomb with great, arching walls and hollows full of skeletons, Sofia came to an abrupt halt before a collapsed tunnel. Ermin, who had been cooing over Corvith, walked straight into the back of her.

'It's just a rockfall,' said Ghino, stopping too. 'It's always been there.'

'Wait.' Sofia was staring at the rocks.

'What?'

But Sofia couldn't speak. As Ghino shone the lamp across the walls, something above her had caught her eye . . . and it filled her with more hope, and more dread, than anything she had seen so far on this dizzying day.

'Sofia?' Ermin was looking at her uncertainly. 'You look . . .'

But Sofia was pointing, and Ermin raised his head too. He gasped.

Ghino turned to them both.

'What?' He shone the lamp on the stones above them. 'What are you looking at?'

Sofia cleared her throat, unable to dislodge the lump stuck there, and answered in a tiny voice, 'Mamma.'

Ghino waved his hand before Sofia's eyes. 'Did you hit your head?'

Sofia pushed his hand away impatiently. 'Look.' She could not reach the small patch of white in the rock, but it was clear what they were. A series of cogs inlaid into the stone. Wafer thin. Bone white. And there, attached to the cogs by a metal thread so thin it looked like a crack in a rock, was a boulder. A counterweight.

'Mamma made this,' she said, her excitement rising with her voice. 'She must have. Mamma was here.'

Ghino let out a low whistle. 'Clever.'

'Genius,' said Sofia. 'That's what Mamma is.'

'Why?' asked Ghino. 'Why did she put them there?'

'I don't know,' Sofia replied. The tunnel seemed to hold a different quality of air, seemed to be sucking her forwards. 'But we need to find out.'

Sofia pulled the thread, setting off the counter-weight attached to the cogs, and the largest stone in the rockfall swung up, as simply as opening a door. Ahead of them was another tunnel.

'*Che cavolo*,' murmured Ghino.

Sofia snorted. 'What does cabbage have to do with anything?'

Ghino flushed. 'How have I never seen this?'

'You weren't looking properly,' said Sofia. 'Only I'd recognize Mamma's work anywhere.'

'And me,' added Ermin. 'What now? Do we go home or . . .'

But Sofia knew going home was impossible now. There was a new plan. A plan to follow where this path of Mamma's led.

'We go this way,' she said. 'We have to.'

'I don't *have* to do anything,' muttered Ghino.

'Go then,' said Sofia, trying not to give away that she was bluffing. Without Ghino's lamp, they'd be lost. Ghino stared her out until Ermin sighed, like a tired old man.

'Well?' he said.

'Fine,' said Ghino sourly, but Sofia could tell he was excited by the way his eyes flashed.

She took the lead this time, and Ghino gestured for Ermin to go ahead.

'Close the door,' said Sofia over her shoulder. Ghino shook his head.

'No way,' he said. 'Never cut off a possible exit, that's the first rule of living underground.'

Sofia opened her mouth to argue, but Ermin stayed her with a hand on her wrist. 'No one's following us, Sofia.'

'Fine,' she muttered. 'Pass me the lamp then.'

She soon regretted not having her hands free, as the tunnel began to narrow almost instantly. In no time they were crawling and Sofia had to transfer a ruffled Corvith from her arm to her back, where he sat down between her shoulder blades. She could feel him grooming himself, snapping his beak as she pulled herself forwards along the ground.

Fright was hammering through her chest but at least it distracted her from the thought of how small this space was, how much weight was above them – the whole city hovering over their heads . . .

Almost.

'You all right?' she called back.

'I am,' said Ermin shakily and squeezed her ankle, the only part he could reach.

'I don't know why we had to go this way when we were so close to the route out,' said Ghino. 'At least hurry up.'

Sofia ground her teeth. It was very well for him to say – he was used to scurrying around down here like a rabbit.

'I'm going as fast as I can,' she said. 'Corvith's not happy though.'

'No-so!' confirmed the crow.

The walls began to run with beaded water, soaking into their clothes, and the air chilled to the point that Sofia lifted the collar of her tunic so Corvith could shuffle underneath to rest against her skin and keep warm.

The passage widened and narrowed at almost every turn, as though they moved through the belly of a snake like a meal of dormice, which at that moment felt no more fantastical than the reality.

At last the ground changed from stone to dirt, which made crawling less painful. Here and there Sofia could see through the mud to rock, pale and gleaming. She scratched it with her fingernail.

'Chalk,' she said. 'These are chalk hills.'

'Where's all this water coming from?' asked Ermin.

'We're near the river,' said Sofia. 'We must be.'

'I've heard there is a secret river below the hills,' said Ghino excitedly. 'A blessed, hidden river. I've never come this close to it before!'

'The current sounds strong,' said Sofia. 'So why are the wells in the city so empty?'

'I've no idea,' said Ghino. 'Keep going.'

Sofia rotated her sore neck, her hair swishing at Corvith who snapped at it impatiently. 'All right Cor,' she said, reaching over her shoulder and letting the crow nip at her finger.

They rounded an upwardly curving corner and suddenly the tunnel filled with a rushing sound. Sofia flinched – if water found them here, the tunnel would fill in no time.

But instead of being engulfed by a torrent of water, Sofia found herself on a ledge. She wiggled into a sitting position, her legs out before her. She inched forwards and her feet slipped over a drop. A gasp escaped her lips.

15

It was a cavern, as big as their bone house. The walls were dripping water and, illuminated by the lamp, tinged a dancing blue by the rippling pool at the centre.

'Look at this place,' Sofia whispered, pushing herself off the ledge and landing clumsily on the chalky ground.

It felt unspoilt and special, like a natural church. It took Sofia back to the first time she visited the cathedral, the vast space echoing with prayers and the smell of incense heavy in the air.

Here, the only sounds came from a spring just above the pool – faint, tinkling whispers, as though the water was talking, calling her. She walked closer, her fingers tingling. There was a rope secured to a rivet at its edge, trailing into the water.

The pool seemed very deep, its blue changing from light to dark to black. She wanted to trail her fingers in it, to dip her sore feet, to sink into the murky depths . . .

She could see bubbles rising to the surface and carved into the white chalk around the curve of the pool were three words: *sorgente della santa*.

'Look,' she breathed, and felt Ermin scrunch up behind her. '*Saint's Spring*.'

Corvith took off from her back, squawking his displeasure at the hard landing. He flapped his ungainly way round the space, sore wing obviously fully healed, and settled on a ledge about halfway up the wall.

The air in the cavern felt cleaner, less stifling, and Sofia took deep, cleansing breaths, stretching her lungs and body. She hoped there would be no more crawling. Ghino approached the pool, her amazement mirrored in his dark eyes.

'Have you ever been here?'

Ghino shook his head.

They searched for more signs of Mamma but the only hint she, or anyone, had been there was the writing about the water's edge and the rope beside it, leading to depths, the colour of a winternight sky.

She knelt beside the pool, the ground damp beneath her, knees cupped by imprints in the soft rock where someone had knelt before. She ran her hands over the marks and noticed more, pitting the surface round the edge of the pool. Almost as if many people over many years had knelt here in prayer. Perhaps Mamma had been one of them. It was the same in the cathedral, the steps surrounding the saints' relics dipped by decades of knees.

She leant over the water and again the tingling in her fingers began. Her reflection wavered in the surface as her breath hit it. She was a dark shadow, her hair slicked down with sweat, claggy with dust.

She pulled on the rope, expecting a bucket to rise from the watery depths, but it appeared fixed and immovable. She dipped her hands into the pool, and the water was so cold it sucked the warmth from her fingers. She gathered a palmful and drank, the cool liquid hitting her throat like a breath of icy air. It was sweet and delicious, like the water from their well at home and the same sort of calm she felt there washed through her.

'Is it good?' asked Ghino. She looked up. His cloth had slipped off his chin, showing his scarred face, and his expression was stretched open and alight with wonder. Sofia was not so shocked by his appearance this time. It was different, but weren't all faces? She looked away quickly, not wanting to make him feel uncomfortable, and nodded. He dropped to his knees beside her. She realized he was trembling.

'You've really never been here?'

'No,' he said, 'I never knew this place existed.' He pointed at the writing. 'What does that say? And no, I can't read. So if you're going to make fun of me, just go ahead.'

Sofia flushed. 'I wasn't going to.' The truth was, she probably would have done. She was starting to realize that she thought of herself as better than Ghino, and it wasn't a nice thing to think.

'Saint's Spring,' she said.

Ghino leant over the pool, so close he looked like he might topple in. 'So this water is blessed?'

Sofia shrugged. 'Maybe. Someone believes it is.'

Ghino reached down and splashed his face a few times. Then he ran his fingers over his scars and

Sofia realized he was feeling if the water had faded the marks.

'Worth a try.' Ghino sighed heavily and cupped some more water to drink. Together they sat, drinking handful after handful of fresh water.

'Well,' Ermin said, elbowing them apart and plonking himself down between them. 'What now?'

Sofia turned her attention back to the surface of the water, still again now aside from the trail of bubbles at its centre. Ghino held the lamp out over it, and the light funnelled down to the far-off bottom.

'What if it's another way?' She tugged on the fixed rope again. 'Another way out of here.'

'What?' asked Ermin.

Sofia indicated the pool. 'Here.'

There was a pause, and then Ghino burst into nervous laughter. 'You've lost it.'

Sofia glared at him. 'The writing, the rope. They're clues, like the cogs.'

'They can't have been left by your mamma?' said Ghino incredulously.

'That rope must go somewhere.'

'So?'

Sofia looked back to the pool. She was so sure that Mamma was leading them on – and if not Mamma, then something only Sofia understood. The path was meant for her and it felt important, the most important journey of her life.

'So,' said Sofia, hauling a courage she hardly felt into her voice, 'let's find out where.'

She began to slip off her shoes.

'No way,' said Ghino. 'That's mad! We can just go back the way we came.'

'But we came this way because of Mamma's route,' said Sofia. 'We can't stop now.'

'We can—'

'Shush!' said Ermin, holding up his hands. He pointed to Corvith, still high up on the wall. The crow was very still, beady eyes wide, his feathers twitching.

'What is it, Corvith?' hissed Sofia. 'Is someone coming?'

Corvith took off, gliding back along the passage that had brought them to the spring. Sofia's belly flipped. If someone was coming, there was nowhere to hide.

'What are you doing?' said Ghino nervously.

'Going in, obviously,' she said, standing in her tunic and underthings.

'I can go,' said Ermin. 'I'm a better swimmer.'

It was true. When Mamma had taught them in the lake outside Siena, before the smallpox came, Sofia had been too old to really take to it the way Ermin could. Her brain was already too full of thoughts of what could go wrong. Her little brother had charged into the water squealing, and within minutes was swimming alongside Mamma as though he'd been born to it.

'Little otter,' said Mamma, laughing. 'Come on, swan.' She called Sofia this because she tried to keep her neck long and high out of the water while she furiously paddled beneath the surface.

But this water was different. It felt like coming home, even sitting beside it. The thought of diving in should scare her, but she felt only a sense of calm settling over her like a blanket.

'No,' she said in answer to Ermin's question. 'I'll go first. I'm taller, and stronger.'

'I'm not doing it.' Ghino swallowed. 'I can't

125

swim. And I can't hear anyone coming. Maybe your crow's just paranoid.'

'He's not.'

Ghino did not take his eyes from her face. 'You shouldn't do this. It's dangerous.'

Sofia laughed hollowly. 'And crawling beneath the city isn't? Bring the lamp.'

Ermin did so as she sat on the edge of the pool, her feet trailing into the water. Her toes immediately burnt in that strange way skin does if something is too cold, like the body makes itself fire to stop you realizing you're freezing. The pool glowed a lighter blue and Sofia stared down, hoping to catch a glimpse of the bottom.

'Wait,' said Ghino, flapping about. 'Are you sure about this?'

But Sofia knew there was no other way she could go. She was sure Mamma had been here, sure that Mamma had written these words, likely placed this rope. Sofia was determined to find out why.

'I'm sure. Now shut up, we're running out of time to find out what's down there.'

Both boys stood back, biting their lips nervously. They looked like baby birds watching their mother leaving the nest, or maybe like parent birds watching their baby take its first flight.

Sofia didn't give herself time to think about it. She leant forward, shuffling off the edge of the pool and into the water.

16

The pool clenched round her body like an icy
fist, and the breath Sofia had taken was
knocked from her chest. She kicked up, arms so
cold she did not immediately recognize air from
water until she felt Ghino's hands grip her wrist
and steady her palm on a rock.

'Are you all right?' Ermin was peering into her
face as she spluttered.

'F–f–fine.'

'This is ridiculous,' said Ghino. 'You haven't even
gone under properly yet. I really don't think—'

But Sofia did not give him a chance to finish. It
was too cold in the pool to waste time. She pushed
off the rock and bent her body, diving down and
kicking, churning the water and following the rope
into the depths.

Almost immediately, she felt a current swirl round her arms and then her chest. She descended further, her ears popping with the pressure. The current caressed her legs but she tugged herself free and opened her eyes.

She looked up, her eyeballs aching with the cold and her ears throbbing. She was not so deep, perhaps two metres down. Above, the surface was a circle of light ruptured by rocks and the dark outlines of Ghino and her brother.

She took firmer hold of the rope and kicked off again, pumping her legs harder and keeping her eyes wide open.

The water was clear enough to see her arms in front of her, but not enough to spot the bottom. She jarred her wrist painfully on a strange surface pitted with holes and too smooth to be rock, with a current swirling powerfully round it. Her lungs began to burn and she kicked back to the surface, gasping.

'Are you all right?' asked Ghino.

'Something's down there. I just ran out of air.'

She turned her back on them and dived again – kicking down, down, until she reached the bottom once again.

She widened her eyes, hooking her foot under a rock to hold herself in place, and brought her face right up close to what she could now see was a grate. She tried to lift it, but it was bolted in place.

The holes were too regular for it to be anything but man-made. As Sofia hooked her fingers through it, she realized she had been wrong – it was woman-made. And not just any woman: her mamma. It had to be, because the grate was not metal, or wood, but bone. A lattice of locked ribs, so perfect it took Sofia's remaining breath away.

She didn't want to return to the surface but she did, her heart sending warm blood fast round her body, so excited she didn't even feel the cold.

'A grate,' she gasped. 'A bone grate.'

'Mamma?' said Ermin.

'It must be.'

'Is it beautiful?' said Ermin.

'Of course.'

'You two are weird about bones, huh?' said Ghino.

Sofia ignored him. Her heart thudded louder. Mamma must have been here. But how? And what was below the grate?

Corvith came wheeling from the passage. 'So-so!' He flew to the pool, flapping round the cavern. 'Go-so!'

'There are people!' she gasped. 'People coming?'

Corvith ducked and dived, his panic confirming it.

Only Ghino seemed unaffected, watching the crow with disinterest. 'What people?'

'What does that matter?'

Ghino shrugged. 'They might be able to help us, tell us what this place is.'

'Ghino,' hissed Sofia. 'Are you mad?'

'How long do we have?' asked Ermin desperately.

'Push in that rock,' she said, nodding at the boulder beside him. 'It'll get me down there faster.'

As soon as it began to tip, Sofia filled her lungs with the biggest breath yet and grabbed hold. She and the rock plunged. She let go just before the boulder hit the bottom to save her fingers getting crushed, and held on to the grate. She felt quickly round the sides, conscious of her breath already straining at her lungs, and, as she'd expected, found nothing.

Her mother had many mechanisms for fixing things in place. Locks were her favourite, but sometimes a customer wanted a hingeless box and Sofia would watch her mother hiding her workings with even more skill than usual.

'People are used to feeling the edges,' Mamma would say, 'they never suspect the way in is at the heart.'

Sofia felt her way to the centre of the grate and hooked her finger into the centre square. She pushed right: nothing. She pushed left, and felt a sliding. She braced her foot against the rock and pushed harder, her lungs starting to burn. She felt, rather than heard, the click and the ribs of the grate concertina'd on invisible hinges, like a broken spider's web.

She began to spin as the water formed into a vortex, pulling at her feet, and she was suddenly above it, gasping in air. Corvith was shrieking over her head, helpless.

'What's happening?' she heard Ermin shout, and then Ghino's answer: 'The water is draining!'

'Spread your arms!' Ermin shouted to Sofia.

She did so just in time. As her legs were pulled

through the hole left by the bone grate, her fore-arms hit rock. Her scrambling feet searched for purchase underneath and at last her right foot wedged into a crevice. She pushed herself up, her foot twisting viciously with the effort. It felt as though her ankle bone had been yanked out of place and put back together almost before she registered the pain.

As the last of the water disappeared, Sofia hauled herself out of the hole.

'Are you all right?' called Ghino, his voice shaking.

'Just about,' she called back. Ermin was crying, and she could see Ghino wrapping his arm round her little brother as claws tightened on her shoulder.

'So!' Corvith nipped at her ear, chittering with worry.

Sofia reached up and stroked him, as much to calm herself as the crow.

'It's all right, Corvith. Look, I'm all right.'

But she was not entirely sure it was true. Her ankle felt like it had its own heartbeat, too hot and too cold all at once. It was flushed, a bruise already rising.

She peered down into the hole, Corvith gripping on tighter to her shoulder. It did not go much deeper. She lay on her belly, her head dangling. It was too dark to see much and she waited for her eyes to grow used to the gloom.

'What's down there?' called Ghino.

She could see nothing but the black hole where the water must have gone.

'How did her grate get there?' asked Ermin shakily.

'Mamma must have put it there herself,' said Sofia, staring at the grate. 'She was keeping it a secret. No one would know what this was.'

No one except Mamma, and Ermin, and her. She felt an enormous lifting in her chest. *We're coming, Mamma. If you're at the end of this, we'll find you.*

'We're out of time,' Ermin gasped.

She looked up, but he was not looking at her. His and Ghino's faces were underlit by the lamp, and she could see the line of their chins tense.

'Ermin?'

'Shhh!'

A moment later, he extinguished the lamp.

Plunged into sudden and absolute darkness at the bottom of the drained spring, Sofia was barely able to breathe.

She could hear a scuffling. Ghino let out a yelp of surprise.

'Move out the way!' called Ermin.

'Ermin . . .' Sofia began, but a moment later Ghino was tumbling gracelessly down the rope with Ermin close behind. They landed with a thump, in a heap beside the open grate.

'You pushed me!' said Ghino indignantly.

'What, were you going to stay there and let them catch us?'

'We don't even know who they are!' snapped Ghino. 'I bet they'll be impressed with what we've found. They might give us a reward.'

'Are you mad?' hissed Sofia, horrified. She groped for Ghino in the dark and took a firm hold of his arm.

'Hey!'

'Shut *up*!' She clasped her hand over his mouth. She couldn't believe how stupid he was being. Ermin helped her bundle Ghino down into the black hole beneath the grate before jumping down after him. Water sloshed round their ankles, and Sofia peered down at them and into the dark. A tunnel stretched ahead.

Ghino made as though to stand, but Ermin sat on him to keep him still.

Sofia fought the impulse to laugh at the expression on Ghino's face . . . until she realized it should be impossible to see anything at all this far underground.

The people Corvith had sensed were here, and they had a lamp.

17

S ofia braced herself, lowering her body as gently
as she could, but still she landed with a jarring
thud on her injured ankle.

'Are you really all right?' murmured Ermin. He
was watching her closely. She nodded, impatiently
wiping away tears. She reached up to close the
grate, but Ghino bucked Ermin off. 'No! The first
rule—'

She shook him off. 'Don't be stupid,' she hissed.
'They'll catch up. What is *wrong* with you?' She
drew the grate closed until it clicked and locked
into place. 'Come on.'

They stood before the dark maw of a riverbed,
and somewhere there was the faint sound of
rushing water, though the water round their ankles
was stale and moving sluggishly. Sofia's whole body

felt tingly now, the warmth of her blood fighting the chill of the tunnel.

Sofia wished they could light their lamp but the voices were becoming distinct now, grunts as many boots hit the cavern above them. The glow from the lamps washed through the grate and Sofia and Ermin drew Ghino deeper into the shadows.

'Well?'

Sofia held her breath. That was a woman's voice – Sister Rosa's voice, this time Sofia was certain of it. 'No sign of anyone, Capitana Rosa,' replied a guard.

Ermin clutched Sofia's hand, mouthing, *Capitana?*

Inching out of the shadows, Sofia peered up through the grate. Sister Rosa stood at the edge of the saint's spring high above. Sofia could see her clearly this time, but she was no longer dressed in a nun's habit.

Sister Rosa wore a fitted, belted silver tunic and the trousers Sofia had seen when she had climbed into the cart. But this was not the strangest thing – Sister Rosa carried a sword in a scabbard that hung from a knotted belt at her waist. A guard's sword.

Sofia's head spun. She had been right in thinking there was something suspicious about this woman. Sister Rosa was not a nun at all.

She was a soldier.

'I definitely heard something,' said Capitana Rosa. 'Water, and voices.'

'There's water dripping from the walls,' said the guard, longing clear in his voice. 'It must be the hidden river—'

'I'm well aware of that, you oaf—' Capitana Rosa broke off, and Sofia heard astonishment in her voice. 'Look at this. *Saint's Spring*. What is this place?'

They had obviously never been here before, so how had they reached it now? Sofia groaned inwardly. The open rockfall. This was Ghino's fault. She shrank back as the lamp was held over the empty pool. Ice entered Capitana Rosa's voice. 'What's that, at the bottom?'

'I'm not sure, Capitana Rosa.' The guard whistled and they heard a crack of wings as his magpie took off from his shoulder, landing a few moments later on the grate with a dull *clink*. It tapped at the grate with its beak and Corvith trembled, burrowing deeper into Sofia's arms.

'It's definitely something, Capitana,' said the guard.

'Definitely *something*.' The woman's voice was scathing. 'How clever. You'd better check what exactly.'

There was a shout, and the sound of air moving fast through clothing. Sofia stifled a gasp as she realized Capitana Rosa had pushed the guard into the empty spring.

She braced herself, ready for the crunching of bones that would surely come when he landed, but he obviously managed to grasp the rope before he crashed heavily on top of the grate. His magpie flapped noisily out of the way.

'Well?'

Sofia heard the guard gasping for air, winded by his landing.

'It's a grate,' he managed between shallow breaths. 'Made of some strange wood. White wood.'

'Can you open it?'

They heard the guard straining with the effort of trying to lift it. 'No, Capitana Rosa. It's fixed tight. Perhaps it's just a drainage system.'

'But who,' said Capitana Rosa snippily, 'put it there? And why?'

'I don't know, Capitana. It's made of something strange. Bone maybe?' The man's voice trembled. 'Why is it bone? Are they the saint's bones? Is that why...' The man swallowed hard. 'How will I get up?'

'The bone builder,' hissed Capitana Rosa, with such venom in her voice Sofia's hair stood up on the back of her neck. 'It must be.'

They heard footsteps, and the lamplight receded. The magpie took off with a snap of wings, abandoning its post on the guard's shoulder.

'Capitana? Capitana!' The guard called out, panicked as darkness slipped around him. But Capitana Rosa was gone.

Ghino backed away from the spring, all desire to reveal them seemingly forgotten.

'Who's there?' whispered the guard hoarsely. 'Please. Help me.'

Ermin tugged on her hand. Sofia felt caught, frozen by pity. But she allowed Ermin to pull her away into the darkness, keeping behind so he would not see her limping. And beneath her cold, and fear, was a small spark of hope. Capitana Rosa had spoken of Mamma.

The woman had lied about not knowing her. But more vitally, Mamma was alive. And Capitana Rosa knew where she was.

18

They walked in near silence until the whimpers from the guard had long vanished. Ghino at last lit the lamp and held it up before them.

'She's beastly,' said Ermin shakily. 'Even to people on her side.'

Ghino was mute, his hand trembling, sending the lamplight skittering across the walls. Sofia wanted to tell him off for leaving the rockfall open, but he looked too shaken to shout at.

The riverbed was slimy with algae, and the pain in her ankle was worsening. She bent to check it, and saw the bruise already blossoming more fully.

Ermin's stomach gurgled. 'I'm *hungry*,' he whined. 'I need to eat.'

He flopped down dramatically on to the sodden

floor, splashing slimy water everywhere.

'Don't you have anything?' snapped Sofia unfairly.

'Only these,' said Ermin, pulling from his pocket a handful of glue beads. 'I took them from the workshop.'

Sofia ground her teeth impatiently, but the truth was she was hungry too. Dinner at the orphanage felt like days ago. She turned to Ghino.

'Well?'

He looked at her blankly. 'What?'

'Did you manage to steal any food on your latest visit up top?'

'I have these,' he said in a dignified sort of voice. 'And I didn't steal them, I made them.'

He dug about in his pocket and pulled out some sort of biscuit, broken into several pieces. 'I think I fell on them.'

Sofia couldn't help but think they were probably improved by the fall. They looked awful – lumpy and grey-brown. They sat down beside Ermin, Sofia lowering herself gingerly, as Ghino held the biscuit pieces out for inspection. They looked as unappetizing as the glue beads.

'What are they?' sniffed Ermin, poking at them with his finger.

'Root biscuits,' said Ghino cheerfully, picking one up and biting into it with difficulty. He sounded like he was chewing on gravel.

'What sort of roots?' asked Sofia suspiciously, as he tipped one into her hand. It was alarmingly heavy.

'All sorts,' shrugged Ghino, now attempting to break one in half for Ermin and Corvith to share. 'Anything I can mush up.'

Sofia didn't want to ask what else he mushed it up with. She took a nervous bite. It felt like her teeth were going to snap and, once she succeeded in breaking a piece off, it sucked all the moisture from her mouth. It was like chewing rock dust.

'Well?' said Ghino expectantly, looking from Ermin to Sofia and back again.

Ermin smiled politely, but Corvith snapped his beak angrily and turned his haughty head away.

'It's not exactly easy to make food down here,' said Ghino defensively. 'You can always eat that.'

He pointed at the wall, slimy and dripping.

'Algae?' Sofia wrinkled her nose.

which reached all the way to the opposite bank. And there, vanishing into dark, was a set of stone steps, cut deeply into the white rock and disappearing out of sight.

Was it still their mother's trail? How had she managed to make all this? It would have taken years, a lifetime. Sofia found the source of the chain, set just below waist height. She yanked on it. There were rivets sunk deep into the rock, and none budged as she pulled. She looped her sore ankle over it, testing if it held her weight. The chain stood firm.

Ermin knelt down beside the river, and Corvith squawked and buried himself deeper into his pocket while Sofia held on to Ermin by the scruff of his collar. 'Careful!'

Sofia's heart thumped. One slip and they would be lost and, even if her ankle were not hurt, she would not be able to kick against the torrent.

She pressed her eyelids tight together, trying to calm her breathing. She had to be brave. For Ermin and Corvith. For Mamma.

Something tickled the end of her nose. Ermin was holding up a sprig of lavender beneath her nostrils. Sofia stared at it, amazed.

'Where did you get that?' She took it tenderly. In this dark place where nothing grew, it seemed a miracle.

'Home,' said Ermin. 'I've been keeping it in my sleeve since Sister – Capitana – Rosa came to collect us, so if I got scared I could smell it.'

'Is this the first time I've looked scared?' laughed Sofia.

'No,' grinned Ermin. 'But it's the first time you've looked more scared than me.'

She breathed deeply. Its purple scent was like the press of Mamma's hand to hers. 'Thanks.'

'Do we have to pull ourselves across?' Ghino asked. If Sofia looked worried, it was nothing like the terror on Ghino's face. She could swear his knees were actually knocking.

'It's easy compared to living down here all on your own,' said Sofia. 'We can do this, Ghino.'

More than that, she thought. *We have to.*

19

Corvith didn't want to leave them, and Sofia had to all but shove him from his perch on Ermin's shoulder. He soared to the other side with the lamp clamped in his beak, buffeted by the wind and spray, and landed on the bottom step.

'I'll go first,' said Sofia, trying to keep the shake from her voice. 'Don't start coming across until I'm off the chain, all right?'

Kissing her locket for courage and without giving herself too much time to think about it, Sofia took hold of the chain. She brought her legs up to hug it, so that she dangled like a monkey, and, swinging, began to edge out over the freezing spray.

The water seemed to leap up at her, sucking and pulling her hair before yanking it free of the braid Capitana Rosa had made when she was still a kind-seeming nun. Sofia forced herself not to think of what would happen if she lost her grip.

Her sore ankle throbbed but she bit back the pain and focused on one hand over another, the movement of her arms, then her knees, inching her forwards until she was at the centre of the river. Her neck ached and she swung it left and right. She snatched a glance below her.

It was a mistake. She caught sight of the churning, black water and her heart began to beat doubly fast. Her ankle pulsed too, and suddenly slipped free.

'Sofia!'

Ermin's voice was tiny against the roar of water. Her ankle sank into the river, the current taking grip and pulling. It should have hurt, but Sofia felt nothing – the cold numbing it and sending tingling traces up her leg.

For a moment she thought she heard the water murmur again, a watery language set beneath the hiss and thunder, and she thought how wonderful it would feel to let go of the chain and allow herself to be carried away.

'Sofia!'

Ermin's voice came again, louder this time, and to her horror Sofia felt the chain dip. She looked to the bank. Ermin was on the chain and edging determinedly towards her, Ghino too paralysed by fear to prevent him.

'Go back,' she cried, but the water swallowed her voice as the chain dipped again. Sofia imagined the links coming apart, breaking, sending Ermin and herself into the watery depths. She gritted her teeth and swung her leg free of the current. New urgency propelled her forwards until she felt the bank scrape her back. She let go of the chain.

Ermin was not far behind. His face was sweaty despite the chill of the water and he collapsed into Sofia's side, his narrow ribcage heaving.

'I told you not to do that,' she shouted into his damp curls, squeezing him tightly.

'I thought you were going to fall,' he said exhaustedly into her shoulder, and she rocked him side to side like Mamma would have. She wished she could stay like this, holding him, keeping him safe, but she had brought them too far on this path to stop now. The only way was onwards.

Sofia let go of her little brother and stood carefully.

Her ankle was tingling, but the pain had receded. The bruise had vanished, her skin was its usual light brown and the nub of her ankle bone was smooth and painless.

'That was awful,' exclaimed Ermin. He looked to the opposite bank. 'Where's Ghino?'

Sofia wheeled round. She could not see him. Was it possible he'd been swept away?

Her panic eased as she saw Ghino's hands emerge from the foaming torrent, followed by his gasping face. She and Ermin must have weakened the chain, because it hung much lower in the water. Ghino clung to the slick metal, bobbing on the surface like a cork, tossed this way and that.

'Careful!' cried Sofia. 'Hold tight!'

Her heart hammering in her throat, she watched as he continued to inch towards them. More than once his weight dragged the chain down to the level of the water and Sofia could see him panicking, spluttering.

'It's all right,' she called, trying to keep her voice steady. 'Just keep going.'

He came hand over hand but as he reached the middle, there was a crunching sound loud enough to be heard over the river. Ghino looked back, eyes wide, scarred face stretched in horror, and Sofia imagined the rivets holding the chain in place, rusted by age and water, starting to turn.

'Quicker!' called Ermin. 'Come on, Ghino!'

Ghino sped up, but it was too late. With an awful grinding sound, the rivets gave way. The chain was sucked sideways, sinking fast. Ghino splashed and gasped, clinging to it as it pulled him down.

Sofia threw herself on to her belly and grasped at the other end of the chain. The rivets were holding this side, but for how long? She scanned the furious water, looking for Ghino's strong arms pulling him to the surface. Nothing. But the chain was still taut and pulling downstream. He was holding on.

'Help me!' she cried and Ermin unfroze, joining her in gripping the rope, and together they began to pull.

Their combined strength was barely enough, but the water was taking some of the weight, and together they hauled the chain until finally Ghino rose from the depths.

Sofia saw that he was not holding on after all.

The broken rivets had caught in his clothing, hooking him like a monstrous fish. His hands lay limp at his sides.

They hauled him up the bank, free from the grasping river. His chest was still, his lips apart, eyes shut.

'Sofia . . .' Ermin's teeth were chattering. 'Is – is he?'

Sofia leant over the boy. He was not, could not, be drowned? She bent to his mouth, willing his breath to tickle her face. Nothing. She brought her hands, trembling, to his throat, to where his pulse should be working quick and warm. His skin was freezing.

'No,' murmured Sofia. 'No, no, no.'

She placed her hands on his chest, where his heart should be beating, and felt the hollow knell of nothing. She leant her weight on to him, feeling for life, coming so close her locket rested on his collarbone and her hair dripped water over his face. *Do not be dead*, she thought. *Don't you dare be dead. Be well, be well, be well.*

'Sofia—' Ermin's voice was reedy.

'Shhh!' She was listening for breath, her smooth

cheek resting on his pox-pitted one. She listened so hard she felt she could have heard into the centre of the earth, to all the worms and other blind things that nested there.

Her hands were pressing so firmly they marked Ghino's dark skin red, the river water from her palms transferring on to his body as she wished and prayed and swore that if only he'd breathe, she'd do anything, give anything. She'd lend her own breath, to fill his chest.

And then, small as a whisper, she felt it; a sharp jolt of something like static pass between their wet skin. A tingle in her fingers. *There*, she thought, *there! Was that* . . .

It was. The small stir of a breath arrived at last beneath her hands. A heartbeat.

'Sofia, he's breathing!'

He was, his chest was rising and falling now, over and over, and Sofia had never realized before how simple a breath was, or how miraculous. Ghino's eyelids fluttered open and focused on her face. Ermin was whooping, his voice ricocheting round the tunnel. Corvith was diving and chittering. But Sofia remained still, and silent, staring at the boy come back to life. She felt exhausted, and more alive than she ever had before.

His dark eyes were bright with river water and tears. 'I'm so, so sorry.'

'For what?'

Ghino rolled on to his side and threw up all over Sofia's feet.

20

After Sofia had rinsed her feet in the river, and Ghino had apologized again, she and Ermin helped the boy into a sitting position. He was shaking and though Sofia comforted him, she felt just as shaky, just as strange. She felt as though her promise had come true: that her breath had been taken and placed precisely into Ghino's chest. She felt winded, outside her body, dizzy with cold.

'Are you all right?' Ghino was looking at her closely.

'Of course she is,' said Ermin dismissively. 'She's not the one who almost drowned!'

'I'm fine,' said Sofia, but the truth was her lungs did feel a little waterlogged – a little too full of something thicker than air. But there was no time to waste, and at least her ankle seemed better. She stood, testing how it took her weight. She could feel Ghino watching her, and wondered if he understood what had happened better than she. Sofia looked at the steps, chalk white and arching out of sight.

'Time to go.'

All three of them quickened their pace, Corvith flying overhead. The steps steepened all the time, narrowing until they were funnelled single file and taking the steps more like a ladder than a staircase, leaning forward on all fours.

Sofia's lungs ached, and she focused on putting one hand before another — hand, foot, hand, foot — keeping her eyes fixed on Ermin's ankles. All the joy of finding the hidden river had faded in the wake of Ghino's near-drowning but now she allowed a glow of wonder to light in her chest, spurring her on. She had to believe Mamma was at the end of this path, together with the truth she had promised Sofia on the morning of her birthday. Sofia needed answers to questions that multiplied with every minute.

Ahead, Ghino's voice bounced down to them. 'What the—'

'Ouch!' Sofia's head collided with Ermin's foot, and from his exclamation she guessed he'd had a similar experience with Ghino. Corvith took off with a squawk of indignation. Ghino was standing on a platform above them, the lamp held high before him, Corvith wheeling over his head.

Rubbing her scalp, Sofia squeezed past Ermin – coming to stand next to Ghino, so intent on the boy it took her a moment to realize why he had stopped.

They were at a crossroads. Three tunnels stretched out of sight; one to the left, one to the right and one straight ahead. Corvith came to settle on a pillar of stone at the centre of the crossroads, flapping his wings and tipping back his head, giving an almost triumphant caw.

'Ghino, are you all right?' Sofia reached cautiously for his shoulder and he started, sending the lamp's light swinging crazedly across the three dark mouths before them.

The light skittered across Corvith and the stone column, which flashed suddenly white.

Sofia gasped. 'What is that?'

She reached forwards, gently nudging Corvith aside as Ermin squeezed on to the narrow platform beside her.

'*Che bello*,' whispered Ermin. 'That is . . .'

'Incredible,' breathed Sofia into his silence.

Atop the stone column was a shape of bone. She recognized what it represented instantly. It was a hollow replica of Siena's centre, made miniature, small enough to fit in Sofia's two palms and carved entirely from bone. Sofia could not see any joins, though she knew they must be there.

She motioned for Ghino to hold the lamp closer. The detail was extraordinary. At the centre the Piazza del Campo was raked, the surface dimpled as though it was spread with soil as it was for the Palio. Only one thing was missing. The cathedral had minute gargoyles, but its striped tower wasn't there. There was only a slot, as fine as a coin – a gap where it should have rested.

'Did your mamma make that, too?'

Ermin hushed Ghino's question, as Sofia placed her hands either side of the model and made to lift it from the base. It would not move. She twisted it, thinking it might be screwed into place, but it stayed resolutely still, as though it had grown out of the rock itself.

'It won't budge,' she said, teeth gritted in frustration. She stared at the model, willing it to reveal its purpose. Corvith settled on to her shoulder and pecked at her pocket until he caught hold of the locket's fine chain.

She drew it out. 'This?'

The crow blinked his bright eye and pecked at the locket again.

'What do I do, Corvith?' she asked.

'Why are you asking the crow?' sneered Ghino.

'Shush!' said Ermin. 'He's clever. You'll see.'

Corvith hopped on to the bone model and jabbed his beak at the cathedral – at the gap where the tower should be.

Sofia understood at last. With trembling fingers, she aligned the locket with the slot and slid it down. It clicked, unmistakably the noise of something finding its rightful place. Sofia tried to lift it again, but still the model would not come away.

Ermin reached past her and pressed at the model's right edge. Soundlessly, in a steady, easy movement, the model turned left. As it did so the locket swung down, like an arrow, pointing to the left-hand tunnel.

'*Che cavolo!*' whispered Sofia.

'Now who's saying cabbage?' said Ghino with a smile.

'It's a compass!' Ermin whispered. 'See? That's the way to the cathedral.'

Sofia pushed the model back the other way and this time the magpie tower swung down, arrowing straight ahead. 'And that's the palazzo.'

She turned it once more, to the right-hand tunnel, and two tiny gates opened. The gates they had to take to leave the city.

'And that,' said Sofia, catching on, 'is the way home! Ermin, Ghino. We have to go this way!'

'*Che bello,*' murmured Ghino. 'Your mamma really is a genius.'

'I know,' agreed Sofia, but the truth was she had never realized just how much. She turned the model back to its original position, and the gates closed. Her locket popped out of its slot and she plucked it out, thinking it more beautiful than ever before.

'Come on,' she said, making for the right tunnel. But Corvith squawked and blocked her path.

'No-so!'

'Yes,' said Sofia. 'That's the way home, Corvith!'

But Corvith was flying back and forth, back and forth, between them and the tunnel ahead.

'We're not going there,' said Sofia impatiently. 'We have to go home!'

'No–so!'

Again, Corvith blocked her way. He flew further up the tunnel, vanishing from sight.

'Sofia,' said Ghino. 'I think we should follow the crow.'

'Are you mad?' said Sofia. 'That's the way to the palazzo!'

'But he's telling us to follow him,' said Ghino. 'And he's the one who showed you how the compass worked.'

'He's right,' said Ermin. 'I think Corvith might know where Mamma is.'

Corvith loomed back out of the tunnel and landed on Ermin's shoulder.

'Is that right?' murmured Ermin, stroking his feathers. 'Do you know where we're meant to go?'

Corvith purred, and Sofia fought back the sudden urge to cry. She knew Ermin and Ghino were right, but she didn't want to go on. She wanted to go home — to be back in their bone house, with their olive grove and their well — where everything made sense.

But only if Mamma is there, said another voice. *That's the only reason it's home.*

Sofia sighed deeply, holding the bone locket tightly in her hand. Then she nodded at Ghino, and said spitefully, 'This is on you if it goes wrong.'

Ghino turned away, towards the tunnel, Corvith flying ahead. 'I'm only following orders.'

They followed the new path, even steeper than before. Sofia tried not to think of what awaited them ahead — a tower of magpies, a palace of guards. *And*, said a small, unwelcome voice, *an impenetrable cell perched on top.*

'Ghino,' said Sofia, as casually as she could. 'Have you ever heard anything about the magpie tower? About—'

'The prison?' he said, almost as casually. 'Yes.'

'A prison?' said Ermin. 'You don't think Mamma is there?'

But Sofia couldn't answer. The truth was, that was *exactly* what she thought. And if Mamma was in that particular prison, it would be impossible to reach her.

Once he was convinced they were obeying him, Corvith settled on her shoulder – his breath coming in nervous little chirrups. As the tunnel widened, a light began to shine from above them, and the crow began to shift from foot to foot.

'Nearly there,' she said, trying to soothe him though she felt as restless and ill at ease. 'It'll be all right.'

'No-so!'

Ghino stopped climbing and turned back to listen. 'Are they behind us again?'

'That's not what he means,' said Sofia, frowning. 'He's scared of what's ahead.'

She looked at the glowing light, and inched closer. The surface of the tunnel began to change. In place of rough rock was seashell mortar, and the steps steepened into a ladder.

The candlelight overhead was sliced by a drainage grate, and Sofia could now see the stone ladder was dotted with black and white.

'Ugh,' said Ermin behind her. 'Is that—'

'Watch your hands,' said Sofia, as the smell of bird droppings started to grow stronger. She smooshed her top lip beneath her nose, the river smell of her skin strong. 'And be as quiet as you can.'

It was almost silent above, only faint rustling like paper in a breeze. Corvith was trembling in her pocket, but Sofia could do nothing except carry on. She climbed to the stinking, stained metal and blinked up into a tower full of magpies.

21

There were hundreds of the birds, perched on the railing of a massive spiral staircase that twisted all the way to the top.

All the magpies Sofia could see were asleep, their beaks folded back between their wings. If she pressed her cheek against the filthy metal, she could see lamps attached to brackets on the floor.

And high, high above, was what seemed to be the night sky, dotted with stars. A painted ceiling of royal blue and gold.

'What can you see?'

Ghino's murmur made her jump and lose her grip on the slimy step momentarily. He was up close behind her, trying to peer through the grid too.

'Magpies,' she replied shortly. She couldn't see

anyone in the tower aside from the birds.

'Any of Mamma's signs?' Ermin asked, squeezing on to the top step too and pressing his nose against the grate. 'Pooh, it stinks!'

'Poo does stink,' said Sofia. 'And keep your voice down!'

She tried to scan the tower, but it was difficult with Ermin and Ghino taking up half the looking space. 'There's no guard.'

'He'll be outside, won't he?' said Ermin. 'They wouldn't expect people coming from down here.'

Sofia looked up again at the dizzying ceiling. This was where Mamma's bone trail had led them. They could not stop now, but Sofia was afraid. She didn't want to open the grate and risk waking the magpies. Corvith poked his head out of Sofia's pocket and chattered softly.

'What now?' she whispered to him.

But there was a scraping sound, and clods of dust and other things Sofia didn't want to think about suddenly rained down on them. Ghino had swung the drainage grid up. Before Sofia could so much as gasp, Corvith had taken off from her shoulder. As he went he brushed his wings against the chalk walls, coating them in white.

'He's making himself look like a magpie!' Ermin whispered.

Ghino ducked back down beside them as Corvith wheeled out of the grid. 'I have to give it to you, he really is a clever crow.'

Sofia punched him hard in the arm. 'What did you open the grate for?'

'That model didn't lead us here just to look,' he hissed back.

Sofia ground her teeth. She wanted to call after Corvith, to have him safe in her arms again. The sight of him flying past all those sharp-beaked magpies turned her stomach.

Ghino and Ermin pressed up beside her as the bird circled higher.

'Where is he going?' asked Ermin, dancing nervously from foot to foot.

But Sofia had no answer. She could only watch as a couple of magpies snapped their beaks when he got too close, his ungainly wings taking him dangerously near to their perches, but none attacked. Sofia exhaled. Corvith was already halfway up, and he had not been spotted by the sleepy magpies for what he really was.

Corvith headed directly to the painted ceiling. He flew in a sharp circle, and swooped out of sight.

'Where's he gone?' whispered Ghino.

'Shush!' hissed Sofia, chewing her nail with nerves until she realized how bad it tasted. 'The cell!'

And then, suddenly, Corvith was there again. But now he had something in his beak, small and glinting.

'What's that?' asked Ermin. But as Corvith started to fly back down, his chalky wing brushed the filthy upper railing and scattered droppings down the length of the tower. A couple of magpies ruffled their feathers, and one stretched out its wings in a sign of aggression.

'No, no, no,' muttered Sofia. She would never forgive herself if Corvith got hurt again. 'They're waking up!'

The magpie with outstretched wings began to chatter, low and threatening.

'Go back to sleep, you beast,' willed Sofia, her fingers laced through the grid and ready to push it open. But then what? She could not get to Corvith.

'The glue!' Ermin's breath was hot in her ear. 'I have glue, from the workshop!'

He fumbled in his pocket for the clump of glue beads.

Corvith was still hovering above, something in his beak, and the aggressive magpie was circling below him still cawing angrily. More magpies were waking, though none of them raised any sort of alarm. Corvith's disguise was keeping him safe, but for how long?

'The lamps,' said Ermin. 'It's the only way.'

'What if they see us?' said Sofia, stomach clenching. But Ermin did not reply. Instead, he reached past her and pushed open the grid. She snatched at him but he was already outside, slithering flat to the stained floor.

Sofia caught the metal before it clanged shut, keeping it ajar, eyes darting between her brother on the floor and the magpies above. She should follow him, grab him. She should go instead. But fear rooted her to the spot.

'What's he doing?' asked Ghino.

Sofia could only squeak in answer. Now the awake magpies were watching the stand-off above them, and the sick feeling in Sofia's stomach grew as more magpies joined in, circling Corvith who was only discernible by the object in his beak.

'Quickly, Ermin,' she whispered. Ghino's fingers gripped Sofia's, her nails digging into the back of his hand.

Ermin had reached the lamps and opened their glass cases wide. He scattered the glue on to the hot metal, evenly on each, and almost immediately the glue began to melt. Ermin started crawling back, Sofia opening the grate wide and reaching for him desperately.

Now Sofia could smell the melting glue, fishy and sharp, the stench sticking to the back of her throat. Ermin reached the grate and, as she clasped him tightly in her arms, Sofia saw a magpie's eye snap open. It raised its head and looked directly at them. It opened its beak and Sofia cringed, waiting for the alarm call . . .

But it didn't come. Instead, the magpie's head drooped and dropped forwards. The still-sleeping magpies next to it fell sideways on to the planks, all knocked unconscious. She tracked the fumes' progress up the walls as row after row of magpies fell sideways or slumped more dramatically, some sliding down the spiral until they bunched along it like children backed up on a bannister.

'Come on,' she hissed, but Ermin was looking up.

'I have to catch Corvith!' He stood up as the fumes reached the top of the tower and the circling magpies began to swoop drunkenly, some finding purchase on the perches while others started to plummet. One spotted Ermin standing below, arms outstretched, and with its last conscious breath, let loose an enormous screech.

Instantly, there was a startled shout from outside – not a magpie, but a person. A guard. Another magpie screeched.

'Come, Corvith!' Ermin called, and there was loud swearing from outside. Corvith obeyed, diving past the dizzy and unconscious magpies, until halfway down he too went limp as a rag. The object fell from his mouth, and Sofia saw at last what it was.

A finger bone, hinged in brass. Mamma's hairpin. As Ermin scrambled to catch the crow, holding out his tunic so he landed with a soft thump in the fabric, Sofia launched herself out to catch the hairpin. It landed, solid and cool, in her hand and she clasped it like a prayer as the door burst open, a guard charging inside.

Ghino threw himself out of the grate as if to help them.

'Don't, Ghino!' she cried.

The guard's hand reached out and grabbed at Ghino's collar. For one, shining moment, as she and Ermin slid back through the grate and into the tunnel, Sofia thought she saw Ghino slip through the guard's fingers. She held out her arms to him.

But then –

'I have them!' Ghino was waving towards Sofia and Ermin. 'Tell the capitana! I have them!'

22

The world seemed to stop, caught in the trap of Ghino's words. Ermin with the unconscious Corvith, Sofia with her arms straining against the weight of the grate, the guard with his hand tight about Ghino's collar: all as still as statues.

Only Ghino kept talking, moving, flailing against the guard's grip.

'Tell her I did as she asked!' he cried. 'Tell Capitana Rosa I have them!'

Even the magpies, falling from their perches, seemed to stall mid-air. Sofia's blood stilled in her veins as Ghino's yells resolved into words, and his words' meanings battered against her heart like arrows, striking at every tender place.

'Call the capitana!' Ghino was still shouting.

'Take me to her!'

As the guard let go of Ghino, Sofia let the grate drop. The clang shook through to her bones, which felt as soft as feathers, just before more people came running.

'Quick, Sofia!' cried Ermin, snatching up Ghino's lamp in his free hand and skidding down the steps just as a monstrous magpie, huge and horribly familiar, thumped down hard on the grid and began to peck through the holes. It was the magpie who had visited their house, the magpie who accompanied the stranger. But now it was unhooded, free of its leash. It dipped its beak through the grate, caught hold of a hank of Sofia's hair and wrenched it from her scalp.

Sofia cried out in pain and climbed down as fast as she could after Ermin, shrinking into the safety of the tunnel just as Capitana Rosa beat the magpie aside. She threw herself down on top of the grate, scrabbling and pulling, but it was set flush to the floor and she couldn't grip the slick metal. She looked possessed, spit flecking her lips as she called for her guards.

'Rip it off its hinges! Bring axes! Bring acid!'

Sofia shuddered and stuffed the hairpin into her hair so she could go faster. Her whole body hurt, her heartbeat hammering the realization home.

Ghino had betrayed them.

Ghino had led them into a trap.

This thought echoed in her mind as she and Ermin fled, barely leaving room for anything else, so that when they arrived at the crossroads of the miniature city she felt as though she'd walked for seconds or years.

'He's with them,' she gasped, panting. 'He's a liar.'

'Why?' said Ermin in a pale imitation of his voice. 'Why did he . . .'

Sofia grasped his hand. 'We have to keep going. You heard Capitana Rosa. They'll be after us as soon as that grate gives. We have to go.'

'Where can we go?' sobbed Ermin. 'Ghino's helping them.'

'I know,' said Sofia. Her shock was hardening into anger, her scalp stinging where the magpie had ripped out her hair. That beast and Capitana Rosa were working together. Was it the captain who had come to their home all that time ago?

'Mamma is there, isn't she? In the palazzo

prison?' hiccupped Ermin. 'Corvith fetched her pin. Should we go back?'

Sofia felt in her hair and pulled out the hairpin. It was warm now, the brass hot from her body's movement. Something slid into place in her mind, neat as the locket in the model.

'She was,' she said slowly. 'She was there.'

'Was?'

Sofia nodded. 'Not any more. The hairpin, it was cool when I caught it. If Mamma had been wearing it up until Corvith found it, it'd be warm like it is now. Feel.'

She tipped it on to Ermin's palm. 'See? Mamma was kept in the tower. Maybe she even left this, as a clue. But she's not there now.'

'Where then?'

'I don't know.' Sofia cast a nervous glance back at the tunnel that led to the palazzo. 'But we have to get out, get above ground. This is Ghino's domain.' His name tasted bitter in her mouth. 'He knows it better than us and he's going to lead them to us. We have to go somewhere we know.'

'But where?'

Sofia looked at the bone model, at the gates that

had swung open before the right passage. She turned to Ermin, who was still clutching the unconscious Corvith. 'Let's go home.'

23

They hurried along the passage, which inclined softly, and Sofia reassured herself by imagining they were up top — above ground, she corrected herself — and walking home after a market day.

Or, as this was her daydream, she could imagine they were walking back from the Palio — but instead of Mamma fleeing the palazzo and being caught by guards, she'd joined them in the crowd. They'd watched the race, the horses galloping round the piazza and the whole city cheering and joyful. She imagined Mamma's hand, calloused and strong, in hers. She smiled, feeling the sunlight warm on her cheeks.

'Are you all right?' asked Ermin, pulling her back to reality. He was holding the lamp up to her face, peering at her worriedly, and she smoothed the creases of his forehead with her finger.

'Fine,' she said. 'Well, you know.'

He nodded miserably and swung the light back in front of them. 'Look!'

Above them, roots were starting to twist through the soil. Sofia traced one with her finger. It came away damp, and water dripped on to her face. The soil must be thinning – they were rising to the surface. 'Come on.'

They quickened their pace, almost running as they rounded a final turn – and there, solid as the roots, was a trapdoor. Sofia almost sobbed with relief, throwing herself against it. But it wouldn't move, no matter how hard she pushed.

'It's locked!' she said. 'What do we do?'

'Sofia, calm down,' said Ermin. 'Look.'

He reached out and pulled the trapdoor towards him. It swung open without resistance.

'Oh,' she said, and then, following him outside, '*Oh!*'

They were home. Not near home, not just outside the gates with a long walk ahead, but actually *home*. At the twisted tree that marked their boundary, their bone house shining ahead, the hill stretching before them. All about them the olive grove twisted, drenched in a brilliant sunset. They'd been underground a whole day. The trees were alight, their silver leaves burnished bronze.

Sofia's heart felt lighter than it had in days. She turned to look behind them. The trapdoor opened into the hollow trunk of the tree, the tree she had seen every day of her life, and yet never suspected what it concealed. She pulled the trapdoor shut. Its wood was as gnarled as the tree's and it was hidden perfectly by the roots.

'*Che cavolo*,' murmured Ermin, and Sofia did not even tell him off for using Ghino's phrase. 'Why does it lead here, to our house?'

'Mamma,' said Sofia. Mamma must have known this was here. She had built the bone house and knew every inch of this hill. Sofia felt dizzy with the secrets, piled atop each other, burrowing through the foundations of what she thought she knew.

She quickly scanned the road. There was no sign of anyone coming after them, but surely this would be the first place Capitana Rosa would look? They could hide in the grove if anyone came, and Corvith could keep watch. But then what? They could not go on like that for ever, not with Mamma still missing.

Ermin was stripping handfuls of olives from the trees, stuffing them into his mouth and spitting pits into the air. In his arms, Corvith was stirring grumpily and Sofia held out an olive for him, too.

'Should we go inside?' asked Ermin, mouth full.

'I think we should wait a bit,' said Sofia, though she wanted nothing more than to lie down in her bone bed and sleep and sleep and then wake from this nightmare. 'See if anyone comes. Let's go to the well.'

Before they started their climb, Sofia tied two of the younger branches of the trapdoor tree together. She didn't think she'd find it again without the marking.

She remembered back to her birthday, three days and a lifetime ago, when they'd left the house only a moment after Mamma and yet not seen any sign of her. She must have been using this passage for years, and she'd never told them.

Sofia began to climb after Ermin, manoeuvring

through the twisting boughs, fresh anger boiling in her belly. Why had Mamma kept so many secrets? Ermin was still young, but Sofia was twelve. Surely she was old enough to be told about things like trapdoors and secret tunnels. Sofia grasped the hairpin, and her anger stalled.

Mamma's face came to her, surrounded by her curls. Her lavender smell, her clever hands, the frown line that furrowed between her thick black eyebrows when she concentrated. Sofia twisted up her hair and stuck the pin into it. She would give anything to have Mamma home.

Ermin was drawing the bucket up from the well. He paused when he saw her.

'You look like Mamma,' he said, nodding at the hairpin. Sofia smiled and slapped her hands together, brushing them the way Mamma always did after a day of bone building, clapping the bone dust from her fingers. Ermin laughed, but there was such sadness in his face Sofia felt it dig straight into her.

'We'll find her,' she said. 'We will.'

Ermin sighed and nodded. He lifted the bucket, drank deeply, then passed it to Sofia. She looked down into the bucket, the water drawn from the hidden river made gold by the sunset, remembering Ghino's cold skin as they pulled him from the torrent, his face drained of blood, his chest breathless. She trailed her fingers into the water, feeling the familiar calm wash through her, and then traced the bone symbol – the intertwined 'R', 'S', 'E' and 'C' on the well – to anoint it like a blessing, a wish that they would be together again soon.

Ahead, the view was the same as ever. Siena's buildings had remained unchanged through all the years of Sofia's life – they knew nothing of Palios and smallpox and missing mothers. The towers of the cathedral and the palazzo pierced the encroaching dark, magpies drawing invisible threads between the two. It was incredible to her that they had been underneath that mighty tower, underneath the city, swooping through, unseen as magpies at night.

Sofia sat up a little straighter. She was wrong. The view was not exactly as it always was. She had never seen the magpies behave like that, flying in deliberate lines from the palazzo to the cathedral.

In fact, there were so many of them, massing round the cathedral spire, it was starting to take on the appearance of a swarm, or storm cloud.

She had hated them when she was younger, hiding under her mother's skirts whenever they visited town. Years ago, before the pox, when Ermin was still small enough to be carried in a bundle on Mamma's chest, Mamma had brought Sofia to the cathedral to see the relics. She'd taken her to a small wooden door at the back of the building.

'The tradesman's entrance,' she'd said with a wink. 'Even God doesn't like the workers coming in the front.'

She'd led Sofia through the door, and into a different world. The crypt was dug before the cathedral even stood, so ancient you could see mosaics from a time when Italy was ruled by emperors, and there were many gods, not just one.

'Like descending through time,' Mamma murmured, leading Sofia through the candlelit dark to a curved room pocked with holes like the inside of a beehive. In each of the holes was a relic, a piece of a saint left behind to grow dusty and more holy with the passing of the years.

'I will make a reliquary for each of these,' said Mamma, patting the sleeping Ermin's back. 'To give them resting places worthy of saints.'

'And when that's done, what will you make?' asked Sofia, believing absolutely that Mamma would make these boxes in no time at all.

'A bone builder's work is never done,' smiled Mamma. 'Unless I could make a skeleton key. Then I would know I'd mastered my craft.'

'Aren't all your keys skeletons?'

Mamma chuckled, her dark eyes flashing in the candlelight. 'Yes, but none is a skeleton key. A key that can open any lock.'

Sofia wrinkled her nose. 'But that's impossible.'

'Bone *is* impossible. It is the only material that could make such a thing. There are locks that need the strength of metal, the lightness of wood, the warmth of life and the cool of death. Only bone has all these qualities. So only a bone builder can make a skeleton key.'

Sofia held her locket tight in her hand. *It matters. Keep it safe.* It seemed to Sofia Mamma had made the impossible possible. But even this wondrous knowledge made Sofia's heart ache. If the locket was a skeleton key, why had Mamma not told her what it was? Why would she not have shared her triumph with Sofia?

'Sofia,' said Ermin, pointing to the massing magpies.

'I know,' she murmured.

Corvith chattered on Ermin's shoulder and he stroked his beak gently. 'What does it mean?'

Sofia didn't want to answer. Once she did she knew her fantasy of remaining at home, pretending all was well, would be over. But she said it anyway.

'It means we wait for dark. We can sleep a couple of hours, but then . . .'

She grasped her locket, the perfect miniature of the cathedral before them. 'It means we have to go back.'

24

The cathedral's pale stone glowed ghostly in the moonlight, the black bands dissolving so it looked like it had been sliced into pieces and sat levitating in the night.

They'd made the journey above ground, thinking it was safer than risking being caught in the tunnels now that Ghino was working against them. The fact they now feared him more than the magpies made Sofia almost breathless with fury. She imagined him leading Capitana Rosa and her guards, pursuing them through the belly of the city. No wonder he'd acted so strangely at saint's spring – if Ermin had not forced him to jump, they would never have got so far.

But then there was his face when the captain had pushed the guard into the empty spring. Ghino had looked pale, afraid. Like he'd finally realized what he had been helping. And now he was in her clutches.

Good, Sofia thought forcefully. It was none of her concern where he was, so long as it was nowhere near them.

It had been the right decision to go above ground. They'd passed no one on the night-time streets, and the magpies still seemed to be concentrated round the cathedral spire. As they drew closer, approaching from a narrow side street lined with bakeries, they shrank further back into the shadows cast by its massive walls.

They'd stayed long enough at home to change their clothes for the darkest ones they owned. They'd even wrapped cloths round their mouths, like Ghino, to avoid the glint of their teeth giving them away. Along with Corvith, the three of them looked like a band of snatchers.

The outfit made Sofia feel safer, and she understood for the first time the strength Ghino took from no one noticing you. She shook her head. She had to stop thinking about him. She wished he'd never existed.

'Nearly there,' she whispered to Ermin, pointing towards the steps ahead.

'We're going the wrong way,' whispered Ermin. 'The entrance is—'

'We're not going in the front,' said Sofia. 'Come on.'

She led them past the jut of the nave, the shunt of the antechamber and up the steep, slick steps at the back of the cathedral. Gargoyles and stone saints loomed above them, their white stone shifting as clouds scudded across the bright moon. Sofia was careful not to look any of them in the eye. They were so lifelike, she was worried they would move.

Finally, they reached the small wooden door at the back of the cathedral – the one Mamma had led her through years before. She pushed it gently open. The moonlight stretched across the mosaic floor, and the relic room sat quiet and curved.

Sofia paused, thinking the sight of these shelves, now full of Mamma's reliquaries, would soothe her. But instead, she saw nothing. She must have gasped aloud, for Ermin pulled at her arm.

'Sofia? What's wrong?'

But she could only point. Every shelf of the curved room was empty. The relics were gone.

Ermin peered in. 'What?'

He hadn't seen it as it had been, couldn't understand the shock she was feeling to see the cathedral's treasures ransacked.

'Sofia?'

She found her voice, tiny in her throat. 'Come on.'

It was almost pitch-black in the transept, like being back underground. Sofia led Ermin towards a meagre glimmer of light. One votive candle burnt solidly in the darkness and Sofia felt her way towards it, feeling beneath its metal stand to find more which she lit from the first.

The reach of the light grew and stretched into the vast space of the cathedral; the quartz floor shot through with shining crystal, shimmering like veins beneath their feet, stretching up a massive font of stone. The walls were crowded with painted figures dressed in robes, staring stern as judges down at them.

The entrance to the tower lay ahead, but before Sofia could lead them any further into the nave the huge doors at the back of the church were thrown open, flooding the cathedral with moonish light.

Sofia dragged Ermin behind the font, peering past the cloth as Capitana Rosa strode inside with – Sofia's heart beat faster with rage – Ghino. But he was being hauled, protesting, his feet dragging on the floor. Their voices carried through the cavernous space, bouncing off the walls.

'I found them, Capitana—'

'Shut up, thief.'

'But I *told* you, the doctor said he would help me—'

'I doubt *he* said anything,' snapped Capitana Rosa. 'And wasn't the deal you would deliver the bone builder's children to me?'

Ermin gripped Sofia's hand so hard it hurt, but she didn't pull away.

'That wasn't my fault—'

'Hush! You better hope the hair is enough to convince the bone builder.'

Sofia cringed as Capitana Rosa held out the hank of Sofia's curls that the massive magpie had taken. She rubbed the sore spot, wondering where the bird was now, as Capitana Rosa pulled Ghino into the antechamber – and soon the voices faded.

Sofia and Ermin looked at each other. 'Mamma,' breathed Ermin. 'Are they going to Mamma?'

'I think so,' whispered Sofia.

Ermin pocketed Corvith, the crow's head swivelling as Ermin ran after the capitana and the thief, bent low between the pews. Sofia followed, heart thudding louder than her footsteps on the flagstones.

Ermin had already slipped into the room ahead, and, full of relief at hearing no shouts of alarm or alert, Sofia hurried after him. She entered a room full of colour, but there was no one inside but her brother and their crow.

25

'W here'd they go?' hissed Ermin.

The room was lit by candles and was only slightly larger than Mamma's workshop at home. The walls were lined with maps, glistening blue and gold and green from glass cabinets. They passed a star chart, spangled in gold and the dotted rotations of the constellations, and a vellum map that looked like an original plan for the cathedral.

Sofia scanned the walls, walking a fast loop round the paper-covered room. She could see nothing out of place, nothing out of the ordinary.

She came to a halt before a huge stretch of parchment, lining almost the entirety of one wall. It alone was uncovered by glass and the design was strange, so Sofia did not at once understand what it was.

The edges were black with channels of white running through them like a termite's nest, twisting and looping strangely. Through the centre ran a trail of brilliant blue, a snake–like curve undulating through the black.

Sofia traced the blue. 'The hidden river,' she murmured. 'Ermin, this is the river we crossed.'

The river Ghino drowned in. Drowned, and yet did not die.

'Sofia,' whispered Ermin. 'Look.'

He brushed the bottom edge of the map. One corner was loose and flapping, as though caught in a breeze. Sofia lifted it. A small wooden door with a bone keyhole, was concealed behind it. She tried the handle, but it was locked.

'Your locket,' said Ermin, but Sofia had already placed it into the keyhole. Pushing the door open, she saw a set of stairs leading not down, but up as far as she could see. Where the palazzo tower had been square, this was circular – an infinite-seeming snail shell, thankfully free of magpies.

Corvith cooed softly, awake now, as Ermin came to stand beside her. 'Do you really think Mamma's up there?'

Though she could not be certain, could not even allow herself to voice the possibility, hope burnt bright and painful in Sofia's heart. Ermin slid his hand into hers and squeezed it briefly before moving past her, on to the stairs.

'Come on.'

The staircase was structured round a stone pillar. It was cool to the touch and there seemed to be something inside it, something whispering and bubbling. Water? Sofia frowned. It made no sense for there to be water here, when the city wells were dry.

Sofia's legs burnt, and her breath came hot and tight in her lungs. They reached a little landing and Ermin stopped, panting and pale. Corvith nuzzled his cheek.

'What's ... that ...' gasped Ermin between great, sucking breaths. He was pointing at a dull wooden door. It, too, had a bone lock, and Sofia looked from it, to the locket.

'Do you think?' Ermin asked hopefully, but Sofia was certain it would not be so easy. Mamma could not be here, behind this door? But just as she was about to shake her head no, they heard a small voice come from behind the wood.

'Hello?'

Sofia had to clap a hand over Ermin's mouth to stop him from crying out.

'Hello?' The voice came again. It wasn't Mamma, or a guard, or even a grown-up. It was a girl's voice. 'Who's there?'

Sofia pressed her eye to the keyhole, but she couldn't see anything. She pressed the locket into the lock, and the door swung inwards.

There, sitting on the bare floor of a tiny dark cell and looking more like a dormouse than ever, was Carmela. Sofia gaped at her, her shock mirrored in the girl's face. Ermin hurried forwards, helping Carmela to her feet. She swayed, unsteady.

Sofia could only think of stupid questions. 'What're you doing here?'

'What're *you* doing here?' echoed Carmela. 'How did you escape?'

'Escape?'

'They're keeping us here. Sister Rosa. And I've seen other nuns, the priest too. They're all soldiers.'

Fear roiled in Sofia's stomach. 'Why?'

Carmela trembled. 'I don't know. But we get moved up through the floors.'

'There are more of you?'

Carmela nodded miserably. 'I've heard them bringing more children. A boy went past just now.'

'Ghino,' murmured Ermin.

Sofia could not allow herself to think about what all this meant. This wasn't about Mamma alone any more. She needed to get Carmela and the others out.

'Carmela,' she said. 'Do you have somewhere you can hide?'

'I don't have a home,' said Carmela.

'The grove,' said Ermin. 'Our olive grove. It's dark. She can make it.'

A plan knitted together in Sofia's mind. It was patchy and full of holes, but they had to help the children.

'Yes,' she said. 'Carmela, take the eastern route out of the city. You know it? Good. Follow it to the highest hill. There's an olive grove there—'

'I don't want to go on my own,' Carmela said, lip trembling.

'Corvith,' said Ermin. 'Our crow can take you.'

Sofia reached up instinctively to the crow. She didn't want him to go.

'We'll be all right, Sofia,' said Ermin. He sounded like the big sibling, not her. 'And we can free the other children on the other floors, and they can all go together and hide while we figure this out.'

Sofia didn't think it would be so easy, and Carmela looked as though she might faint as it was.

'You should come too,' said Carmela. 'It's not safe.'

'Our mamma is here,' said Sofia. 'We have to find her.'

'If I had a mamma, I'd stay too.' Carmela's cold hand found hers. 'Be careful. And thank you.'

They didn't waste a moment more. Leaving Corvith with Carmela, and filled with new urgency, Sofia and Ermin ran as quietly and as fast up the stairs as they could. Soon they reached another landing, another locked door. And sure enough, a boy was behind it.

He blinked at them, astonished. 'Who are you?'

'No time to explain,' said Sofia. 'Take the stairs down, follow the crow.'

She repeated this a further six times, finding a further six wide-eyed, terrified children, before at last, the stairs stopped. They had reached the final landing.

Two doors faced them, both with bone locks. From behind one, voices came low and inaudible through the thick wood. She reached for the handle, but Ermin shook his head. She knew he was hoping Mamma was behind the silent door, that their trail hadn't led them into a room full of guards with no hope of rescuing her.

Though Sofia feared the worst, she opened the other ... and her mouth fell open.

26

At first glance, Sofia saw nothing but white. White ceiling, white floors, white walls. It was the white of brilliant sunlight, so bright it stung her eyes. At first, and even third, glance it looked like the inside of a cloud.

But the longer she looked, the more details emerged.

The room was not painted, but built of polished bone. It was like their home, but larger and more ornate. The walls were braced with femurs, the ceiling a latticework of pelvises. Spines curved at the corners, and the shelves were formed from ribs. The massive, dawn-tinged windows were edged with latches of finger bone. The floor was a series of interlocking knee bones. All the corners curved, lending everything a soft edge, a gentleness. *There are no straight lines in the body.* And there, lining the walls, were the relics that she'd noticed were missing from the cathedral below – each in a brilliant box of bone. She could see Saint Catherine's thumb, mounted in its golden lattice of knuckles and the arm of Saint John, cradled by linked femurs. Each piece was obviously crafted by Mamma, the work too fine to have been made by anyone else. But why had the relics been moved here? Had Mamma brought them?

Sofia clasped the locket in her palm, feeling the familiar pulse of strength bone always gave her. She moved into the white room. It was disorientating, lit by hundreds of lamps so nothing cast shadows. Though the bones were unyielding under her feet she felt more than ever like she walked through a cloud, picking up her feet too high.

At the centre was a well, set flush into the floor like the saint's spring. Sofia peered down into it, surprised to see the water high enough to touch, almost level with the bone-tiled floor. She had been right about the stone column being full of liquid. It was strange to see such a thing so high up, but then Sofia supposed it was the same pressure that meant their hill well could funnel water from the depths. But how could there be so much water here, when just outside the city's wells stood empty? She dipped her hand into the full bucket beside it. It was cool and fresh, recently drawn.

Along another wall, on a table covered in a spotless tablecloth that trailed almost to the floor, lay some glinting instruments so fine she could only just make them out against the pale surface. There were small needles and white thread, soft cotton swabs, and . . .

Her hand trembled. There, amongst the strange objects, was something very familiar.

Mamma's final reliquary. The one she had shown them on the day of the Palio. It was set apart from the others, its hinge clasped.

Sofia slipped her locket into her pocket and reached out to it, barely breathing. But before she could pick it up, the door handle turned.

Sofia did the only thing she could think of and threw herself beneath the spotless tablecloth, dragging Ermin with her. They pressed themselves along the wall, Sofia on her belly so she could just make out the room beyond.

She watched the bottom of the door as it opened, and four people moved inside. Sofia could see Capitana Rosa's boots, two pairs of bare feet and one pair of shoes as light and fine as lace. Sofia caught the scent of mint.

The stranger. Instantly Sofia was hauled into the past, crouching beneath their table at home, as the stranger left, leaving Mamma changed.

Capitana Rosa had not worked alone. The stranger was here.

'Wait outside, Orsa,' said the stranger, and Sofia heard an answering, abrasive caw. The massive magpie who had snatched at her hair. 'And you, kneel by the well,' said the stranger.

Sofia recognized the muddy feet obeying, the skin rough from the tunnels.

Ghino.

'And you can watch, from over there,' the stranger continued, and Sofia saw a figure struggling against Capitana Rosa, dressed in short skirts that skimmed their ankles.

'What are you going to do?'

Ermin could not suppress a gasp, and Sofia clapped a hand over his mouth. That voice! As the figure was dragged past the table, sending the cloth flapping, the scent of lavender overpowered that of mint.

Mamma.

Sofia wanted to cry with relief and fear. Motioning for Ermin to stay where he was she pulled herself forwards a little, using the sounds of Mamma being dragged along to mask it, and peered through the gap to get a better view.

The sun was coming up now, the whole room turning pale gold. And there was Mamma, her dark hair wild and matted without her pin to tame it, her clothes dirty, her eyes large and angry. Relief flooded Sofia's body as she realized Mamma was unharmed, fighting strongly against Capitana Rosa as she restrained her.

Ghino was kneeling beside the well, his scarred face no longer wrapped. He looked tense but excited. And standing over him, was the stranger Sofia had seen at their home. The woman who had begun Mamma's sadness. Her green eyes pierced the scene and were framed by thick pale lashes. But the rest of her face was obscured by a shimmering silver veil, falling like water over her cheeks and mouth, held in place by a delicate silver chain at the centre of her forehead and looping over her ears.

'Is he coming?' asked Ghino excitedly. 'I was promised a cure.' He gestured at his face, its pocked skin. 'A cure when I brought the children.'

'But you didn't bring them, did you?' said the veiled woman.

'I brought others, plenty of children to the orphanage—'

'But not the children I specifically requested. You failed when I needed you to succeed most of all.' She had a very precise way of speaking: a calm that seemed to hold a limitless depth of danger like an ocean, or a thinly covered pitfall. 'You let them get away. I had to rely on Rosa to find them.'

Ermin grasped at Sofia's arm. The woman was lying about Capitana Rosa catching them.

'Please,' said Mamma. 'I told you, we cannot do what you have promised him—'

'Shut up,' said the stranger dismissively.

'But the cure,' said Ghino. 'Please, won't you fetch the doctor?'

The stranger laughed. 'The doctor is already here.'

Ghino looked around in confusion.

'Rosa,' said the stranger, and Capitana Rosa crossed to her. She unlaced the coronet from the woman's head and undid the thin chains holding her veil in place. At last Sofia saw the woman's face.

It was pitted with deep, red holes, raw and angry-looking. There were scars patterning from her neck to her cheeks, leaving only her forehead and the skin about her eyes unmarked, a reminder of her once creamy complexion. But still, Sofia recognized her. The green eyes and the long, silky golden hair. The woman had survived the disease, but her good looks hadn't.

It was Serafina Machelli. The duchessa.

'That's better,' said Duchessa Machelli. 'I can barely breathe with that on.'

'Then why wear it?' snapped Mamma.

Duchessa Machelli laughed. 'Because appearances are everything, oh great bone builder of Siena. Most people don't care what's under the skin, don't care if your heart is true, or your bones strong, as you do. Only how you look on the outside. Especially when you're a Machelli.'

Ermin squeezed Sofia's hand, only just catching

on. He widened his eyes at her and she nodded in answer to his silent question.

'You're . . .' Ghino paused, seemingly fascinated by Duchessa Machelli's face. 'You're like me.'

'I am nothing like you,' sneered the duchessa.

'Maybe the doctor can help you, too,' said Ghino, and Sofia recognized pity in his voice. 'He's going to fix me.'

'You don't need to be fixed, child,' said Mamma softly. 'Don't you understand what you've done, bringing children to her?'

'Silence!' snapped Duchessa Machelli, but a moment later her voice was melodious again as she turned to Ghino. 'You are right, child, that the doctor is doing everything they can to help. That is why you are here.'

'But where is he?'

Serafina Machelli smiled, and the sore skin of her face cracked. 'You're looking at her.'

27

Duchessa Machelli laughed again, a sound like cool water skimming over smooth pebbles. 'Don't look so shocked. Is Capitana Rosa not a soldier? Is this not the great bone builder of Siena?' She gestured at Mamma. 'Am I not the duchessa? So why not a doctor?'

'But . . .' Hesitation was writ large in Ghino's voice. 'If you are the doctor, why have you . . . why is your . . .'

'Why have I not cured myself?' Duchessa Machelli rounded on Mamma, anger twisting her scarred features. 'Because the cure is beyond science. I needed this woman's skills, and yet she sought to keep her gift for herself. She lied and lied and lied, but no more!'

She spat at Mamma's feet, a gesture Sofia would

never have expected from a duchessa. But now she saw she was wrong about so many things.

'I won't,' said Mamma defiantly. 'Because I can't, Duchessa Machelli. I cannot do as you ask.'

'We'll see about that,' snapped the duchessa. 'Why don't we ask your daughter to convince you?'

Sofia froze. Did the duchessa know they were there?

Mamma's voice shook. 'Please, no.'

'Oh, they led us on a merry chase. We caught up with them eventually, though,' said Duchessa Machelli, her eyes intent on Mamma. 'Caught them both in the palazzo's magpie tower.'

Sofia bristled. The duchessa was lying! But there was no way to let Mamma know. Mamma looked breathless, on the verge of tears.

'No,' she croaked. 'I don't believe you.'

'You don't need to,' said Duchessa Machelli. 'I can prove it.'

She held up the lock of hair that the huge magpie, Orsa, had ripped from Sofia's scalp. It throbbed in memory, and Sofia rubbed it soothingly.

'What have you done with them?' Mamma cried.

'Nothing,' said Duchessa Machelli. Her eyes flashed. 'Yet. And if you help me, I'll let them go.'

'I can't,' said Mamma, tears in her eyes. 'Please—'

'Rosa,' said Duchessa Machelli, seeming to lose patience. She was a magnificent actress. If Mamma called her bluff, what would she do? 'Fetch the girl.'

'I'll do it!' Mamma collapsed against Capitana Rosa, all her fight leaving her. A sob escaped but Sofia saw her taking deep breaths to stay calm, just like she'd taught Sofia and Ermin.

Duchessa Machelli smiled triumphantly. 'I knew you would come to your senses.'

The duchessa nodded at Capitana Rosa and she released Mamma. She stumbled forward, eyeing the soldier's blade.

'Don't try anything,' snapped the captain.

'I have brought your final reliquary,' said Duchessa Machelli, gesturing to the table where Sofia and Ermin hid. 'And the water is freshly drawn from the well you made me.'

'Why not you,' said Mamma. 'Why the boy?'

'You know why,' hissed Duchessa Machelli. 'Show me how you heal him, and then you will heal me, too.'

Sofia understood at last. Duchessa Machelli wanted Mamma to heal her scars, as she had healed Ermin of the pox. Why had Mamma not helped her, not agreed to it, and avoided all this? She listened as Mamma lifted the reliquary, her feet close enough to touch.

'Hurry,' said Duchessa Machelli, hunger in her voice. 'The sun is rising. That is the best time, is it not?'

The whole room was burnished and brilliant with colour. How did the duchessa know about Mamma's skills; know that she needed sunrise, and bones and water? The thought of Mamma telling anyone but her family about her gift felt wrong to Sofia.

'You know she's using you,' said Mamma sadly, eyeing Ghino. 'You're an experiment, like the rest of them.'

'The rest?' Ghino stuttered.

'Don't play innocent,' purred Duchessa Machelli. 'You knew we were taking children. You helped me collect them in my orphanage.'

'I thought you were giving them a home. I didn't know . . .' began Ghino, but Duchessa Machelli held up a slim finger.

'Hush! You don't need to excuse yourself. I understand what it is to be shunned for the way you look, to feel like an outcast. In the years since my looks were taken, I have sought a way to restore them. The orphans have been useful to test my methods.'

'This is wrong,' moaned Mamma. 'They're children.'

'Parentless children,' said the duchessa dispassion-ately. 'No one will miss them. No one *has* missed them.'

Sofia's heart was thudding so hard she wondered how they could not hear it, could not feel it shaking the knee-bone floor.

'You're a monster,' said Mamma.

'You think I don't know that,' said Duchessa Machelli, gesturing to her face.

'Not because of how you look. Because of what you've done.'

'You are not blameless,' hissed the duchessa. 'You helped me with this room, with the locks.'

Sofia saw tears on her mamma's cheeks. She longed to run to her, to throw her arms round her. 'You told me nothing of your true plan. I spoke in theory, only. I never thought—'

'I know that's a lie,' hissed Duchessa Machelli. 'You are a visionary, Renata, like me. You are clever. You must have had some idea when you told me what I wanted was perhaps possible, but only with bones, that I would find a way to make it happen.'

'I didn't—'

'Enough!' spat Duchessa Machelli. 'The sun will soon be up. The crowds will come for the Palio. Today I will reveal myself to them, beautiful as a duchessa must be. You delayed this once, but now you are out of time, bone builder. Show me, or I will drown this boy right in front of you.'

She reached down and snatched a handful of Ghino's hair, making him gasp in pain.

'I can't,' said Mamma desperately. 'Please, I can't do it!'

Sofia didn't understand. Duchessa Machelli was tilting Ghino's face towards the water. She was going to kill him and all Mamma had to do was heal him the way she had healed Ermin, the way

Sofia knew she could.

'Fine,' said Duchessa Machelli. 'First this boy, then your girl.'

And she plunged Ghino's face into the water.

28

'N^{o!'} Before she could think, before she could even register her voice leaving her mouth, Sofia launched herself out from the table and straight on top of Duchessa Machelli.

She had the element of surprise. The locket tumbled from her pocket as she knocked the duchessa sideways, freeing Ghino, who lifted his head from the water, gasping.

Capitana Rosa had reacted instantly, drawing her sword, but Ermin was close behind Sofia and he threw himself at the soldier's knees, bringing her to the ground. Her head hit the floor and the sword flew from her hand. Ghino kicked it right into the well. It sank instantly in a whirl of bubbles.

Mamma joined Sofia in restraining the duchessa.

'Sofia,' she gasped. 'I thought—'

'There's no time!' Sofia could hear Orsa scrabbling at the door, cawing to be let inside. 'We have to get out of here!'

But there was only one exit. Capitana Rosa was already stirring groggily, the duchessa was kicking and the giant magpie was battering at the door. They were too high up to jump from the window and there was no way they could swim down the well. They would have to run for it.

'Get her veil!' Sofia shouted, and Ghino darted to the table where the duchessa's veil lay. From all Sofia had heard, she guessed the woman wouldn't follow without it.

'Go!'

Ermin flung open the door as Duchessa Machelli clawed at Ghino, tripping in her desperation to reach the veil. She fell and narrowly avoided the well as Orsa wheeled into the room, screeching.

Duchessa Machelli pointed furiously. 'Attack!'

But they were already out of the door, Mamma slamming it behind. They had a head start, but not for long. Sofia felt like she flew down the stairs, following after Ghino and Ermin with Mamma on their heels as they passed landing after landing, unlocked door after unlocked door. Sofia's heart was leaping from her chest to pound in her mouth, her ears.

Too soon she heard the bang of the door above them as it was flung open, followed by Orsa's screech. The magpie was after them.

They broke out into the map room, tearing right through the map of the hidden river, and into the cathedral.

Now Sofia could hear the crowds, the buzz and chatter of a thousand citizens amassed outside. As they crossed the slabbed floor to the exit, Sofia chanced a look back. The map room door was thrown open, crashing hard against the wall and echoing round the cathedral. Orsa swooped out followed by Capitana Rosa, blood dripping down her forehead and her finger stretched out in an awful admonition.

'Stop them!'

They plunged out of the door. Sofia's head spun as she took in the scene before them. It was like she'd travelled back in time. The piazza was full of people, the ground again packed with soil brought from the surrounding hills, so that the horses' hooves would not have to contend with the hard stone surface of the raked square.

The second Palio was about to begin.

It brought their last visit spinning back and she gripped on to Mamma and Ermin, determined not to be parted from them. Despite herself, Sofia looked round for Ghino and spotted movement coming from a grate set low into the cathedral steps. It was slightly askew, and Sofia watched as nimble fingers pulled it straight. She caught a glimpse of a wide-eyed, pockmarked face staring back at her.

And then, he was gone.

'Mamma,' Ermin panted. 'Where are we going?'

Mamma looked at him desperately, and Sofia realized that their mother had no idea what to do.

Capitana Rosa was snarling behind them as Orsa soared overhead. The giant magpie was gaining fast on them now and Sofia felt a shadow, vast and cold, blot out the sun. She braced herself, imagining armoured talons outstretched, plunging deep into her flesh.

'The magpies!' The cry was tossed round the

piazza, and Sofia snatched a look up.

Corvith was there! Their crow dived down – and trailing him, like a scarf of endless silk, was a flock of magpies. They came pouring from the sky over the palazzo, turning the air shadowy with their wings. Hundreds and hundreds of the creatures, chasing the bird that had escaped them the previous day.

As Corvith plummeted so did they, blocking Orsa's advance. The crowd shrieked and scattered as the feathered mass bore down and as soon as Corvith plunged into Sofia's outstretched hands, Sofia broke the barrier into the Palio arena.

The ground was vibrating, and a quick look to her left showed her why. The horses, startled by the magpies, had begun to run. The trumpeter was desperately blowing, trying to stop them, but the horses were terrified. Sofia looked behind her. Capitana Rosa was forcing her way through the feathery chaos, her eyes intent on Sofia. Beyond her, all was pandemonium. The magpies had their blood up and, as people ran, they dived and scratched, pecked and shrieked. Guards were pouring from the palazzo, and the horses were coming.

Capitana Rosa was only an arm's length away, and behind her a tide of horses closing in.

'Capitana!' she shouted. 'Capitana, watch out!'

The woman could not hear her. As she threw herself towards Sofia, blinded by fury, Sofia only just had time to move out of harm's way before the horses bore down on Capitana Rosa, trampling her into the dust.

29

S ofia was shaking. She could not bring herself to look. Corvith nibbled her ear gently.

'So?'

'Her!' said a guard. 'Seize her!'

Sofia couldn't run any more. She threw Corvith into the magpie-blackened sky. 'Go home, Cor, quick!' Corvith took off, chittering and crying, just as the guards reached her. There was no sign of Mamma and Ermin, but she knew the crow would find them.

She allowed herself to be carried through the crowd and up a massive set of steps. Amid her confusion Sofia saw a set of doors open before her, all her thoughts dark, messy, and tangled as her hair. The palazzo. Would they take her to the magpie prison, to the cell where Mamma had dropped her hairpin?

The guard steered her through the grey stone entrance hall, into a wide room that glimmered gold from tapestries hung about the walls. Around the high ceiling was a thin metal tube, exactly the same as the one in the orphanage. There was a fine oak chair, arranged next to a broad, throne-like seat. Beside this was a table, upon which was set a sliding lever, of the kind she had seen Capitana Rosa use in the sewing room.

There was a deliberate tread on the floor behind them and the guard stood to attention, gripping Sofia tightly, as Duchessa Machelli swept into the room. She had a different veil on now, a gold one, and her eyes burnt into Sofia.

'Sit.'

She gestured at the oak chair topped with an embroidered cushion, and settled herself on the throne.

The guard stood back from the door, and a moment later Orsa soared into the room. The bird was panting, her beak dipped in red. Sofia shuddered.

Duchessa Machelli dismissed the guard. 'Orsa

will handle her if she tries anything.'

He bowed and departed, closing the door behind him. The sounds from outside were extinguished, the fine tapestries cocooning them in silence. Sofia felt as though she was in a cage with a serpent. Though Orsa was the one with talons, this woman's cruelty was sharper than any blade.

Duchessa Machelli removed her veil once more. Just as with Ghino's wounds, Sofia found she was already used to the duchessa's. The woman's actions frightened her far more than her scars. Her mouth was set in a pitiless smile as she dropped Sofia's locket on to the table beside the lever.

'Now, Sofia.' Duchessa Machelli drew out the syllables of her name, musical and threatening. 'You caused quite a commotion just now, killing my captain.'

'I didn't mean—'

'Silence.' She said it quietly, but with such force and venom that Sofia felt winded. Duchessa Machelli tilted her head, a predator considering its next meal. 'Sofia Fiori. Your mamma has told me so much about you.'

Sofia somehow dredged up her voice from

somewhere deep in her belly. 'She . . . she did?'

'No,' said the woman flatly. 'No, she told me nothing about you. I knew she had children, but she never spoke of you. I admired that. I assumed she was a woman like me, a woman who cares not for children and drudgery but for her work.'

Sofia shifted angrily on her beautiful chair. She knew Mamma loved both: she, Ermin and Corvith were just as much a part of her as bone binding was.

'And then,' said Duchessa Machelli, 'I realized she is full of the same frailties as so many of my fellow women. She proved that today – willing to let that boy die to protect her brood.'

'She wouldn't have let you kill him,' protested Sofia.

'She would,' sneered the duchessa. 'You saw it yourself. She did nothing when I near-drowned him. She would not even try to share her gift until I threatened you.'

Sofia could not think what to say. Mamma's refusal sat uneasily with her – she did not understand why Mamma would not have healed the duchessa in order to escape home to them.

'And then I realized,' said the woman calmly,

'that despite all her lies, she told the truth about one thing. She could not help the boy. She could not help me. She is a fraud.'

'She is not!' shouted Sofia, and her voice was swallowed instantly by the thick tapestries. Orsa cawed menacingly. 'She is the finest bone builder in the world. I saw what she did. I saw the room she created.'

'That is not the gift she lied about.'

'What do you mean?'

'Oh, it'll be much more fun if she tells you.' She pulled the lever beside her and spoke to the room. 'Guard? Fetch the bone builder. I'm sure she'll be on her way east, to her home. Tell her I have her daughter. Truly have her, this time. If she does not return immediately, I shall arrest them all and gift their crow to Orsa.'

Sofia could hear her voice reverberating round the palazzo, carried through the pipes. Unlike the one at the orphanage, this had two different slots. One must be for the palace, and the other? She remembered the day of the first Palio, when the disembodied voice had pursued her mamma. The other was to speak to the piazza outside.

'Now, while we wait,' said Duchessa Machelli, stroking Orsa with a long, elegant finger, 'I wonder if you can guess what we have been doing here.'

'Stealing children. Killing them, for all I know,' snapped Sofia.

'I do not waste life without purpose,' replied the duchessa smoothly. 'I value life. I value beauty, and health. That is what my work is here. Your mamma considers herself an artist, does she not?'

'She *is* an artist,' said Sofia defiantly.

'Well, I am something far more important,' said Duchessa Machelli, and her voice was as soft as spider's silk. 'I am a doctor, a scientist. While artists spend their time making fripperies – shallow objects – I decode the world. I *decide* the world.'

'If Mamma's work is so shallow, why are you obsessed with having your looks back?' snapped Sofia.

Pain flashed across Duchessa Machelli's face. 'Because what is a woman if she is not beautiful? What true power can I have when I look like this? It is the way of the world.'

'But you claim to decide the world,' said Sofia. 'Why do you not help change it?'

229

Duchessa Machelli let out a throaty chuckle. 'Some things are beyond changing. You saw how that gutter rat was treated.'

Sofia bristled. Ghino might be a traitor, but he was still a person.

'A defenceless child,' continued the duchessa. 'Cast out because he was too *damaged*.' Her green eyes slid to Sofia's. 'If they will not help a child, you can be sure they will not help a woman.'

'Not everyone is like that. Not everyone judges people by their face.'

'No,' said Duchessa Machelli. 'Your mamma is only interested by what's under the skin.' She rested her slim hand on the locket. 'And doesn't she work marvels. Why don't you tell me about this?'

30

S ofia's heart thumped harder.

'It's nothing.' She shrugged. 'A *frippery*.'

'Do not lie to me, child.'

'It's nothing,' said Sofia again.

'Orsa,' said Duchessa Machelli lazily and, fast as a lightning bolt, the bird launched itself forwards. Sofia barely registered the pain in her cheek before the bird was back on her mistress's shoulder, Sofia's blood dripping from her talon.

'Let's try that again,' said Duchessa Machelli. 'What is it?'

Sofia swallowed, bringing her hand up to her cheek. It was a shallow scratch, a warning.

'It's a key,' she said, settling on a half-truth.

'A key?' said Duchessa Machelli, searching Sofia's face before seemingly deciding it was the whole truth. 'How does it work?'

'I can show you,' said Sofia shakily.

Duchessa Machelli sat back in her chair, considering, and then nodded. 'All right. But if you try anything . . .'

Orsa snapped her beak.

Sofia stood, and walked to the table on shaking legs. She reached out a trembling hand and fumbled for the locket, losing her balance on the rucked edge of the thick carpet. She banged her palm on to the table, righting herself unsteadily.

'Careful,' hissed the duchessa. 'Idiot girl.'

'S-sorry,' stuttered Sofia. She held up the locket. 'It's a key. For the cathedral. See?'

She pointed at the grooves along its edge.

'Clever,' murmured the duchessa. 'I'll have your mamma build me a handle for it. She'll have plenty of time during her life imprisonment. Oh, don't worry,' she continued, smiling unkindly at Sofia's expression. 'You'll be joining her.'

'Me?' Sofia shuddered. 'Why?'

'We'll wait for her to explain.'

'Duchessa Machelli,' said Sofia eventually. 'May I ask you something?'

'So polite suddenly,' said the duchessa, narrowing her eyes suspiciously. 'I do not like politeness. It gets you nowhere and makes people think you are weak.'

'All right. I want to know something,' said Sofia more boldly, and the duchessa laughed her shockingly beautiful laugh again. 'The children. Why did you lock up the children?'

'Children,' said the duchessa, an ill-concealed shudder in her voice. 'Vermin. Always catching colds and fevers. And surviving! So, when the smallpox came I knew I had to contain as many of them as possible, keep them in the orphanage. I stayed off the streets, diverted the water so I would have my own clean supply.'

'But the citizens,' said Sofia, unable to stop herself. 'There's a drought!'

'You can ask your mother about that,' sneered Duchessa Machelli. 'You sound like my late husband. He caught smallpox from children – orphans he was helping in the street. He brought home their disgusting disease and gave it to me before I could lock him away to protect myself.'

She sighed, as if his death was the most terrible

nuisance. 'And then I needed a ready supply of subjects to experiment on.'

'Experiment?' said Sofia in a faint voice, remembering the prisons in the cathedral and the shining instruments on the table in the bone room.

'Science requires sacrifice,' hissed the duchessa. 'The orphanage was perfect. I could lock up children there, take them when I needed them — out of sight, out of mind. I know there's a way to extract their youth, their resilience. I thought the solution might be in their blood.'

Sofia clapped a hand to her mouth, bile burning her throat. She felt sick but Duchessa Machelli spoke calmly, almost bored.

'Rosa and the magpies helped me. She recruited that tunnel urchin to round up strays and bring them to the orphanage. Anyway, my citizens are too stupid to question my authority. They didn't care. Peasants.' The distaste in her voice was horrid to hear. 'My husband was never a true leader. He didn't have the stomach for it.'

At that moment, a guard burst in from outside.

'Excellent,' said the duchessa, reaching for her veil. 'Is the bone builder here already?'

The guard's face was pale. He looked as though he'd been slapped. 'Duchessa.'

Sofia heard his voice echo back at them.

'What?' snapped the duchessa.

'Duchessa,' repeated the guard, his voice a whisper and yet still Sofia heard it as it spread through the palazzo. 'The lever . . .'

And now Sofia heard something else. Shouts, coming from the piazza. Though the duchessa had forgotten a world outside this thickly tapestried room existed, the Palio crowd was still thronging the square. But what Sofia heard were not shouts of joy, or excitement. They were angry voices. And then, hammering began on the large wooden doors.

'What on earth?' said the duchessa. She leant in closer to the lever, and then looked from it to Sofia. She reached out and pulled the lever back.

Her face turned the same shade of red as the blood on Orsa's beak. When Sofia had stumbled, she'd moved it to its second setting. The lever had turned the pipes on, and projected their conversation to the whole piazza.

Duchessa Machelli's lips twisted in fury. 'You!'

She lunged then, faster than Orsa had, something black and terrible in her face like a serpent about to unleash a fangful of venom. Sofia stumbled back, tripping over her chair. The duchessa was almost upon her, hand raised to strike, but at that moment the doors swung open – banging on their hinges and shaking the tapestries from the walls.

In poured the people of Siena. The duchessa was drawn into the angry crowd, as they shouted and shrieked. Sofia caught only snatches of words, all of them furious.

'Our children!'

'The orphans!'

'Evil!'

Sofia was yanked to her feet, and she recognized the guard who had come to tell the duchessa of her blunder.

'Go!' he cried. 'Go home!'

Sofia didn't need telling twice. Snatching her locket from the table, she pushed through the furious mass of bodies and out into the piazza.

31

The journey felt the furthest she'd ever travelled. Behind her, the angry shouts faded and soon all she could hear was her own heart hammering in her ears.

Sofia pounded through the city's narrow streets, past the shops, the tanning pits. It could not be so simple, could it? It could not be that just past the city boundary, next to that familiar hill, Mamma was home?

She stopped to catch her breath as she reached the hill, hands on her knees, heart jumping in her chest. She looked up at their olive grove, and a dozen sets of eyes stared back.

'Sofia!' Carmela ran forwards out of the grove, arms wide to embrace her. Sofia returned the hug and peered over the girl's shoulder to see the other rescued children emerging from the trees, eyes hollow, chewing crusts of bread. Sofia wondered what they must have seen, if any of them had already experienced Duchessa Machelli's experiments. The thought was too horrible to hold.

'You're here!' Ermin's voice rose from the grove, and then he was barrelling towards her. She released Carmela and held him close, Corvith flying excited loops round their heads. 'Mamma was just about to leave to look for you!'

'Sofia?'

There, in the doorway of their house with her arms full of lavender and a bone tucked behind her ear, was Mamma. Sofia's breath stopped, her heart stopped, the world stopped and did not start again until a stem of lavender fell to the floor, then another and another until it all came tumbling down in a tide of purple and green as Mamma threw open her arms.

And then she was running towards Sofia and Ermin, trampling the stems underfoot – the bright, familiar scent was in Sofia's nostrils and in her hair as they collapsed together, Mamma's rough hands clutching them so tight Sofia felt she might never let go.

Eventually, Mamma released them. She did not stop crying though, and laughing, and smoothing their hair and wiping away their tears even as more and more spilt down her own cheeks. Sofia had missed how it felt, to be looked at like that, like she was something rare and precious.

'Mamma?' she asked, as though this may yet be a gift taken away.

'*Carissima.*' She held Ermin to her again. '*Carissimo.* My dear, dear ones. You did so well.'

'Capitana Rosa is dead, Mamma.' Sofia could not stop crying. 'And the people are rioting, and it's all my fault.'

'It is not your fault. You did it all perfectly . . . beautifully.' Though Mamma's words were soft, her face was alight with a fierce love. 'I am so proud of you both.'

'But why, Mamma?' Sofia felt suddenly angry. She shuffled away from the pile of lavender, away from her mother and brother, conscious of the curious eyes of the orphans in the grove. 'Why didn't you tell us what was going on?'

'Sofia.' Mamma reached out. 'I am so, so sorry.' She looked round at the orphans, who had settled back to their meal. 'Ermin, will you fetch our guests more water?'

'I want to—'

'Please,' said Mamma firmly. Ermin sighed and stomped off up the hill.

Sofia turned to Mamma, dry-mouthed. What did Mamma want to tell her that Ermin couldn't know?

'Come inside,' said Mamma, as though Sofia had spoken aloud, 'and I'll do my best to explain.'

Mamma offered her milk and honey, but Sofia couldn't stomach it after their encounters with Capitana Rosa at the orphanage. She sat at their scrubbed table and waited for Mamma to find the way to begin.

Finally, Mamma took a deep breath and fixed her eyes squarely on Sofia.

'What do you remember from when your brother was ill?'

This was not a question Sofia had been expecting. 'Ill? A few years ago, you mean?'

'Three years ago, yes.'

'It wasn't that bad. You healed him.'

'No,' said Mamma. 'He was very ill. Gravely ill.

He nearly died.'

Now it was Sofia's turn to shake her head. 'You took him to the well, and he got better.'

'He had smallpox, Sofia. He was so small, and weak, and he was going to die.'

Sofia gaped at her for a moment. 'Well then, you are an even better healer than I thought.'

Mamma watched her with an intensity that made Sofia squirm. 'I love you both, so much.'

'I know,' said Sofia.

'Love makes people desperate. You saw it, when Capitana Rosa showed me the hank of hair. I would have tried to heal Ghino, even though I knew I could not.'

'You can—'

'Listen. I'm trying to make you understand.' She took a deep breath. 'I could not have healed Ghino, just as I could not heal Ermin. That night . . .' She shuddered. 'We were losing him. I was desperate. The hospitals were full. The doctor who came to our house said nothing could be done. As the sun rose, I decided to try to call the Fiori gift to me. I took him to our well, the well that our ancestors have used for centuries, and tried to make the gift come. I laid my hands on him, drenched him in the water, laid bones on to his skin—'

Her shoulders slumped. 'It wouldn't work. And then, you were there. You'd snuck up to see where we'd gone.'

Sofia could remember now, but it was not the memory as she had always recalled it with Mamma calm and washed in morning sunlight. In this new memory, Ermin was writhing and pale and Mamma was crying, her face frantic.

'Nothing worked. Nothing worked until . . .'

But Sofia didn't need Mamma to finish. She knew, now, what had happened.

She had been smaller, her hands unable to wrap round Mamma's as she tried to comfort her. She remembered Mamma weeping and holding Ermin to her chest, and pulling Sofia to her too. Sofia remembered her brother, wet from well water – remembered resting her hand on his hand and wishing with all her body, all her heart, all her blood and soul and bones, that he would live and be well. And hadn't there been something small and delicate in her hands, as thin as a wafer, pressed against his chest?

Mamma smiled sadly as Sofia looked up at her, her eyes blurring with tears. She remembered now, that feeling she had when Mamma gifted her the locket. Like she'd held it before.

When Sofia spoke, it was both a question and something she realized she'd always known.

'You didn't heal him,' she whispered. 'I did.'

32

'Nothing worked until I touched him,' said Sofia, her voice gaining strength. 'I . . .'

'Saved him,' finished Mamma. Sofia slumped back in her chair, the memory of Ermin's illness carrying her back to the tunnels, to the moment Ghino had not been breathing and then suddenly had.

'I'm a bone binder?'

'More than that – you are a healer. The strongest in our line, perhaps since the first Fiori breathed.'

'And you . . .'

Mamma sighed. 'I am not.'

'Why didn't you tell me?'

'I thought it was too much responsibility,' said Mamma. 'You were so young and I had never known power like it, in all the generations of Fioris.

It frightened me, knowing what might happen if people found out you could pull people back from the brink of death. You saw what Duchessa Machelli did to me, keeping me imprisoned.'

'But you helped her!' said Sofia. 'You built that room. I know you did.'

'I didn't know what she needed it for,' said Mamma desperately. 'I thought she only wanted something beautiful, somewhere peaceful to live out her mourning. She asked me to help channel the river, so she could bathe in it daily.'

'Why did you do that?' asked Sofia.

'I convinced myself she had good reason,' said Mamma. 'I felt sorry for her, being trapped by what other people thought of her.'

'The children in the orphanage—'

'I didn't know,' said Mamma sadly. 'Please believe me, Sofia. I am guilty of ignorance and allowing myself to be flattered by such a woman, but I am not cruel. You must know that.'

'Why didn't you tell anyone?'

'The river,' said Mamma, her face creased with remembered anguish. 'The hidden river of Siena. She discovered that I'd been channelling the river into our well too, to keep Ermin healthy.'

Sofia could not believe what she was hearing. 'You did what?'

'I know.' Mamma looked wretched. 'She said she would tell you, and I knew you would never forgive me. You are better than I am, Sofia. You would have told me it was wrong to keep the water for ourselves.'

She hung her head. 'The day before your birthday I finished my final commission, the reliquary. I thought she was trying to harness the power of the relics. I told her I would not help her any more, but that's when she told me she had a second secret to hold over me. Worse even than the river.' Mamma swallowed. 'She told me she knew about Ermin surviving.'

'How?'

'The doctor,' said Mamma. She looked exhausted, but Sofia was not done with hearing the story yet. 'The doctor who came to see Ermin, who told us he would not survive. He told her about the boy brought back from the brink of death. The whole thing had been a trap. She'd been making me build the room to imprison me in. She was going to keep me there, going to use the power of the relics and the water to heal her, to stop her ever falling ill again. To carry out more experiments . . .'

Mamma trailed off, the pain in her face so clear that it was obvious she knew what the experiments involved. And yet, Mamma had helped Duchessa Machelli. Sofia knew this would have been her fate if Mamma had not protected her. But still she could not forgive the lies, the way Mamma had helped the plan, trapped the river. Not yet.

'I'm sorry,' said Mamma. 'I wanted the deception to end. But instead it unravelled further. I still can't believe I put you in so much danger. You should never have been in the tunnels.'

'Ghino took us,' said Sofia with venom. 'He was working for Capitana Rosa and the duchessa.'

'Don't blame him too much,' said Mamma sadly. 'He has no family and believes his looks to be a curse.'

'Then why did you offer to cure him? Even when . . .' *Even when you could not.*

'I would have tried anything, while I thought you were in danger.'

'You might have hurt him,' said Sofia accusingly.

'Love is dangerous,' said Mamma. 'It makes you selfish. Makes you blind to all others.' She looked at Sofia. 'You would have thought I'd have learnt my lesson, but there is still nothing I would not do for you.'

Though Sofia was still angry, the tight bud of annoyance in her chest loosened slightly. She understood a little of what Mamma was saying. She would do, had done, anything to keep Mamma safe. Even followed a thief on a trail into the belly of their city, crawled through tunnels, braved magpies and hidden rivers.

'How did you make all the things we saw in the tunnels?' she asked. 'The counterweights, the grate?'

'The Fioris have used that river for centuries, taking the sick there to heal at the saint's spring. It is not all mine. I merely maintained the grate and the cogs. But I added the model, to show the way home.'

Sofia thought of the imprints in the chalk, the press of many knees. How she'd felt it was like a church – and it was, of a sort. The church of the Fioris. But she would not let them keep it for themselves any longer.

'The river,' she said. 'We have to release it. We have to fill the wells again.'

Mamma nodded. 'We need a special key for that.'

Sofia met her mother's gaze. 'Mamma, did you give me a skeleton key?'

At last, Mamma nodded. Sofia slumped back in her chair, this final amazement knocking her breathless as she reached for her locket. 'I can use this to free the river?'

'Not quite. You need the handle.'

'Where is it?'

'Here,' said Mamma, and drew out her hairpin from Sofia's curls. The pin Sofia had made all those years ago. 'I designed the locket so only this makes it a true skeleton key. Go on. You should do it.'

The hairpin was warm in her hand as Sofia felt for the tiny hole in the locket's side she had noticed at the Palio. The joins were so fine it took Sofia two attempts to slide the hairpin in. There was a little *click*, and suddenly the locket opened in an entirely new formation. It looked nothing like the locket any more, its halves rotating away from each other and back, like a book with a cracked spine.

'*Che cavolo*,' she whispered and instead of chiding her language, Mamma laughed.

'I am rather proud of it,' she said.

'But why make it at all?' asked Sofia.

'To control the river,' said Mamma. 'When Ermin was sick, I diverted it and never gave the water back. I put my family above so many others. But you will right my wrong, Sofia. I raised you to be a better person than me.'

Sofia held the locket up to the light. 'Show me how.'

33

Ermin caught up with them as they trudged up the hill, the orphans distracted by a game of catch played with olives.

'Well,' said Ermin. 'What's been going on?'

Mamma and Sofia looked at each other and laughed. It was such a simple question, with such a difficult answer.

'What's so funny?' said Ermin.

'It's up to Sofia,' said Mamma. 'It's her story as much as mine.'

'When you're old enough,' said Sofia. Ermin shoved her gently as Corvith landed on her shoulder. 'All right!'

She told him as briefly as she could all that Mamma had revealed to her, saving her gift until last.

'You saved me?' gasped Ermin.

'Yes, so you can do my chores for the rest of your life,' said Sofia.

'I saved you plenty of times in the tunnels,' said Ermin. 'I think we're even.'

'Fine,' said Sofia, sticking out her tongue. But she was more nervous than she seemed. The locket was smooth in her hand, the familiar finger-bone hairpin warm from her skin. It seemed impossible that this, so small and lovely, would undo some of the damage Mamma and Duchessa Machelli had done.

But after all, hadn't she and Ermin saved the children? Hadn't they found Mamma and exposed the duchessa for what she really was? Small things could change the world. She would never underestimate herself again.

'Here we are,' said Mamma, tapping the well. Her fingertip brushed the place where their initials intertwined: 'R' for Renata, 'S' for Sofia, 'E' for Ermin and the 'C' for Corvith that Sofia had etched there when she was younger. Sofia brushed her fingers into the water, feeling the power pulse through her. She had a gift, just like Mamma – but unlike Mamma she was going to share it. She wasn't going to keep it only for herself and their family.

She lifted the locket and pressed it at the point where the letters overlapped.

The bone outlines clicked downwards. Sofia twisted the key and the bones rotated, moving into a new formation like a flower or a whirlpool. There was a sucking sound, as there had been when the saint's spring emptied.

Their well began to drain and Sofia imagined she was carried on the tide of released water, watching as all Mamma's and the Fioris' clever hinges and cogs turned. She imagined rockfalls, like the one they'd encountered, rising with dams giving and the tunnels filling. She almost felt the joy of the water as it flooded its rightful paths, draining the cathedral tower and washing away all the sin that had been done there – the bone city compass sinking as the well levels rose. Relief rushed through her, cool and tingly and as right as a lock finding its key.

'That's it?' she murmured.

'That's it,' said Mamma.

'Look!' Carmela called.

Sofia shielded her eyes and saw a sight she had never seen before and would never see again.

From the city came two great waves: one of people running on the ground and another of magpies, swarming the sky. She tilted her head back as shadows flooded overhead.

The magpies were fleeing, led by the huge shape of Orsa, and below their feathery canopy a lone figure rode a massive white horse. Sofia shielded her eyes and looked closer. Even at a distance, Sofia could recognize the glint of a veil. Duchessa Machelli was being chased from the city.

The orphans cheered as they watched her, the citizens dropping their pursuit as she pounded across the fields and disappeared into a fold in the landscape. Sofia hoped she would never enter Siena again, or any place where she could wield her power to hurt.

'What'll happen now?' asked Ermin.

'We can tell the citizens the orphans are safe,' smiled Mamma, pointing at the crowd, which now moved towards their hill. 'They'll fetch them and take good care of them.'

'And then?'

'The wells will fill and we'll have a new leader. A kinder one.'

'You can't promise that,' said Sofia. She knew she could not stay angry at Mamma for ever, but she couldn't let her lie any more or make promises she couldn't keep.

'No,' said Mamma. 'But we can hope.'

'And then?' said Ermin.

'Things will go back to normal,' said Mamma.

'No,' said Sofia, her fingers still tingling from the well water as she slipped the locket back round her neck and handed Mamma her pin to tuck into her curls. Mamma took it and twisted up her hair.

'It won't be normal ever again,' continued Sofia. 'But that's all right.' She stroked Corvith. 'Maybe it'll be better.'

As they made their way back down to their bone house, the ground beneath the ancient boundary tree shifted. Sofia leapt back as the concealed trapdoor was thrown open and a dark figure emerged, spluttering.

'Ghino!' gasped Ermin, running forwards to help him to his feet. 'Why are you here? You're all wet!'

'The tunnels,' coughed Ghino. 'The tunnels are

filling with water. There I was, minding my own business, when this great wall of water comes spilling over me and carries off my root biscuit!'

'I think you did him a favour there,' winked Ermin at Sofia. But Sofia's face was set in a scowl.

Ghino did not have time to say a word more before she shoved him, hard.

'Sofia!' snapped Mamma. Ghino looked crestfallen as Ermin hurried to help him up again.

'He betrayed us,' hissed Sofia. 'He would have let us be caught and killed if it meant getting what he needed.'

'It's not true, Sofia,' said Ghino urgently. 'I never would have let them hurt you—'

'But they would have! You see what monsters you were helping?'

'I didn't know!' He grasped for her hand but she pulled away. 'I only wanted to look . . . normal. I only wanted to not have to hide any more.'

'Sofia,' said Ermin. 'I think we should forgive him.'

Sofia crossed her arms. She could not believe she had wasted some of her gift on saving this boy. He looked up at her like a kicked puppy and something in her softened.

'I won't forgive you.'

His eyes filled with tears.

'Not yet, anyway.' Sofia turned to Mamma. 'I was thinking, we might need more help now that your workshop is open again.' Mamma smiled. 'Corvith fitted in well enough. Maybe we could have another orphan in the house . . .'

The hope on Ghino's face was so painful Sofia felt a loosening in her chest, a thawing in her heart. 'You'll have to do my chores for a month.'

'Sofia!' chided Mamma, but Ghino nodded eagerly.

'For a year, if I have to.'

The duchessa was right about one thing, Sofia thought. Being polite was not always the way to get what you want.

'And you'll have to promise not to hide your face any more. There's nothing wrong with it.'

'If you say so,' said Ghino, but he was smiling.

Sofia sighed and pulled Ghino into a tight, if somewhat damp, hug.

'Welcome home, thief.'

ACKNOWLEDGEMENTS

I always start by thanking my family, so this time I want to begin by saying the hugest, heartfelt thank you to my Chicken House family. Six years ago, I joined the coop and have been allowed to spread my wings in the most marvellous ways.

To Barry Cunningham, for taking a chance on this wide-eyed book-hugger. To Rachel Hickman, for beautiful covers and endless encouragement. To Elinor Bagenal for many happy memories at book fairs, and finding my stories homes all over the world. To Kesia Lupo, for her loveliness and friendship (and brilliant books). To Laura Myers, for her ceaseless patience and cat chats. To Jazz Bartlett Love, for her deep enthusiasm and generosity (and always a spare pen). To Esther Waller for making it always smooth sailing and calm seas. For Sarah Wallis-Newman, for style tips and kindness.

And of course for my editor, Rachel Leyshon — wise, generous, and annoyingly, achingly always, always right. Thank you for it all. For six years (and many more to come) of launches, conference calls, editorial emails, and boundless space for our stories to grow. A thousand times over, thank you.

Thank you to my agent Hellie Ogden, for being a constant champion and friend through the best, and the hardest, of times. Thank you to all the team at Janklow & Nesbit, UK and US.

Thank you to my mum Andrea, my dad Martyn, and my brother, John. You know it's all because of you. Thank you to my grandparents. It's quite a lot because of you, too. Thank you to my aunts and uncles around the world, and to my cousins. To Sabine especially, always. Thank you to Oscar and Luna, for trapping me at various writing desks.

Every book is enabled and inspired by my friends and family. This one began with a postcard from my mother-in-law Janis, saying 'In the grounds of the ruined monastery, there was a charnel house.' Thank you to her and Piers for opening Italy up to us. Thank you to my brothers- and sisters-in-law, and to my niblings Tilly, Fred, Emily, Pippa, Isla, and Ted.

Thank you to my best friends Sarvat Hasin, Daisy Johnson, and Tom de Freston. For writing, and for everything else.

Thank you to Jess, and Jessie, and Jess: the precious Jesses. Thank you to Lucy Ayrton, Paul Fitchett, Matt Bradshaw, Robin Stevens, David Stevens, Laura Theis, and Nick Myers, my Oxford family. Thank you to all my friends, especially the Tiffin Girls' survivors, for advice and alcohol.

Thank you to Katie Webber, Kevin Tsang, and Evie Webber Tsang – wonders, all. Thank you to Maz Evans, Lucy Strange, and M.G. Leonard, the best of hens. Thank you to all my Chicken House author pals.

Thank you to Anna James, and Katherine Rundell for the adventures. Thank you to Sophie Anderson and her family for wild swimming and wilder tales. Thank you to Samantha Shannon, Melinda Salisbury, and Alwyn Hamilton for friendship and ferocity. Thank you to Onjali Raúf, Ross Montgomery, Patrice Lawrence, Krystal Sutherland, Sita Bramachari, Emma Carroll, Nikesh Shukla, Jessica Townsend, Katherine Arden, Elizabeth Macneal, and Jessie Burton, for their support and their stories.

Thank you, reader, for choosing this story. It's yours, now.

Thank you to the twins, for making your mark briefly, indelibly, beautifully. How lucky we were.

Thank you to my husband, Tom. I love you much, I love you most.

Kiran Millwood Hargrave

Since the publication of her debut novel, *The Girl of Ink & Stars*, in 2016, Kiran Millwood Hargrave has proven herself to be one of the most exciting voices in children's fiction. Her books for children and young adults include *The Island at the End of Everything*, *The Way Past Winter* and *The Deathless Girls*. Her debut novel for adults, *The Mercies*, was a *Times* number one bestseller and chosen for the Radio 2 Book Club.

Kiran lives in Oxford with her husband, the artist Tom de Freston, and their rescue cat, Luna.

kiranmillwoodhargrave.co.uk
@Kiran_MH